V

Hesitates

He wondered how many policemen were inside there, and then he wondered if he should go in. Maybe it was too early to be bothering them. He walked up some fifty feet to where there was an entrance break in the low stone wall, and then walked into the park and onto the gravel path paralleling the stone wall. He looked across the police station again, and then sat on a bench with his head partially turned so that he could watch the building...

He supposed he would have to talk to a detective. That was probably the thing. You probably went in and said you wanted to talk to a detective, and they probably asked you what it was in reference to, something like a bank or a business office, he supposed.

He didn't like the idea of talking it over with somebody before they let him see a detective. That bothered him a little. He wanted to see a detective right out and clean, get it over with...

Also by Ed McBain

Ghosts
Ten Plus One
See Them Die

About the author

Ed McBain is one of the most illustrious names in
crime fiction and a holder of the Mystery Writers
of America's coveted Grand Master Award. He
has written more than eighty works of fiction,
including the heralded 87th Precinct series and
the acclaimed Matthew Hope series. His real name
is Evan Hunter, and he lives in Connecticut with
his wife, Mary Vann.

He
Who
Hesitates

A Novel of the 87th Precinct

CORONET BOOKS
Hodder and Stoughton

First published in Great Britain in 1965 by Hamish Hamilton Ltd
Published in Great Britain in 1994 by Hodder & Stoughton,
a division of Hodder Headline plc.

10 9 8 7 6 5 4 3

A CIP catalogue record for this title is available from
the British Library.

ISBN 0 340 59331 8

Typeset by Phoenix Typesetting, Ilkley, West Yorkshire.

Printed and bound in Great Britain by
Cox & Wyman Ltd, Reading, Berkshire.

Hodder and Stoughton
A division of Hodder Headline PLC
338 Euston Road
London NW1 3BH

This is for Elaine and Albert Aley

1

When he awoke, the windows were rimmed with frost and the air in the room was bitter cold. He could not remember where he was for a moment. His bedroom back home was always cold on a winter's morning, but this was not his bedroom, and for a moment he grappled with its alien look and then remembered he was in the city. He got out of bed in his underwear and walked swiftly across the wooden floor to where he had put his clothing on a chair the night before.

The room was sparsely furnished. A bed was against one wall, a dresser on the wall opposite. There were two chairs in the room: the wooden one over which his clothes were hanging, and a stuffed easy chair near the curtained window. There was a sink in the corner, but the bathroom was in the hallway. He sat on the wooden chair as he tied his shoes, and then walked quickly to the sink, where he began washing. He was a huge man, six feet five inches tall and weighing two hundred and ten pounds. His hands were immense, brown and calloused like a farmer's. He soaped his face, and then scooped up water from the sink, splashing it onto his massive nose and high, chiseled cheekbones, his full mouth and roughhewn chin. He rinsed the soap away from his eyes and then opened them and stared at himself in the mirror for just a moment. He reached for the towel and dried himself.

He supposed he should go to the police.

God it was cold in this room.

He wondered what time it was.

He walked swiftly to the chair and pulled on his shirt and buttoned it, and then slipped his tie under the frayed collar without tying it, just letting the ends hang loose on his shirt front, putting his heavy tweed jacket over it, and then crossing his long arms in front of him and slapping his sides to generate a little warmth in his body. He went to the window and pulled back the yellowed lace curtain and looked down past the FURNISHED ROOMS sign to the street two stories below, trying to determine the time by the number of people awake and moving around.

The street was empty.

He knew he should go to the police, but he didn't want to go barging in there at six o'clock in the morning – well, it was probably later than that. If it was only six, it'd be dark out there, wouldn't it? The street was empty only because it was so damn cold, that was all. He wouldn't be surprised if it was nine, maybe ten o'clock already. He let the curtain fall and then walked to the closet and opened it. A small and very old suitcase rested on the floor of the closet. The suitcase belonged to his mother and there was a single sticker on it, a yellow and green one with the words NIAGARA FALLS, NEW YORK in a semicircle and a painting of the falls in white and blue in the middle of the sticker. She had gone there on her honeymoon. This was the only piece of luggage she had ever owned, and she gave it to him each time he came into the city to sell the woodenware. He usually came maybe three, four times a year. This was the first time he'd come in February.

He remembered all at once that tomorrow was Valentine's Day.

He would have to send his mother a card.

He took his heavy green overcoat out of the closet, the one he always wore to the city during the winter months, and carried it over to the bed, dropping it there. He went to the dresser and picked up his small change, which he put into the right-hand pocket of his trousers, and then picked up his wallet, looked into it, and then removed the money he had got yesterday for the woodenware. He counted the money again – it was exactly a hundred and twenty-two dollars – and then put it back into the wallet and went to the bed again, and picked up his coat, and put it on, his massive shoulders shrugging into the air as he performed the operation.

He buttoned the coat, then walked back to the sink and looked at himself in the mirror again. He looked all right. He didn't want the police to think no bum was walking in there.

He wondered where the police station was.

He would have to ask the landlady, what was her name?

If she was awake.

He was hungry too. He'd have to get him some breakfast before he went to the police.

He wondered if he should pack the few things he'd put in the dresser or wait until later. He supposed it would be all right to pack them later. Maybe he ought to mail the money to his mother, though. That represented a lot of work, that hundred and twenty-two dollars, a lot of work. And it had to last until maybe April or May when he'd be coming to the city again – well, when his brother would be coming, anyway. Yes, he'd pack later.

He went out of the room, locking the door behind him, and went down the steps to the first floor. The linoleum on the stair treads was old and worn; he had noticed that when he'd taken the room two nights ago. But the reason he'd come all the way uptown here for a room was because he knew it'd be a lot cheaper than a hotel. So he wasn't about to start complaining about the worn linoleum, hell with that. So long as the bed was all right and didn't have anything crawling in it, why that was good enough for him. He was only paying four dollars a night for the room, you couldn't do much better than that unless you wanted to go down to Skid Row, he wasn't about to go sleeping with a bunch of drunken bums.

The landlady's apartment was on the ground floor at the end of the hall. The hall smelled nice and clean, she'd been scrubbing it on her hands and knees the day he'd taken the room, that was Tuesday. He'd known right off it was going to be a clean place without any bugs in the bed, that was the important thing, the bugs. Don't take no bed with bugs in it, his mother had said. He didn't know how you could tell if a bed had bugs in it until you got into the bed with them, and then it was probably too late to do anything about it, they'd eat you alive. But he figured the smell of that disinfectant in the hallway was a sure sign this lady was clean. She probably used something on the coils of the bedspring too, that was where the bugs hid. His mother always washed out the bedspring coils back home with a toothbrush and ammonia, he didn't know why ammonia, but he supposed it killed anything that was in there. Sometimes she sprayed them, too, with some kind of bug killer. She was very clean.

He wished he knew what time it was because he didn't want to get the landlady out of bed if it was too early in the morning. Well, he had to tell her he was leaving today, anyway, settle up with her. He lifted his hand and tentatively knocked on the door.

"Who is it?" she said.

Good. She was awake.

"It's me," he answered. "Mr. Broome."

"Just a minute, Mr. Broome," the landlady answered. He waited while she came to the door. Somewhere in the building, upstairs, he heard a toilet flush. The door opened.

"Good morning," he said.

"Good morning, Mr. Broome," the landlady said. Dougherty, that was her name. Agnes Dougherty, he remembered now.

"I hope I didn't wake you up, Mrs. Dougherty," he said.

"Nope, I was just having my breakfast," she answered. She was a small, thin woman wearing a faded wrapper imprinted with primroses. Her hair was in curlers. She reminded him of his mother, small like that. Don't ask me how I ever give birth to a young horse like you, his mother always said. It *was* kind of funny, when you thought of it, her so small.

"What was it you wanted, Mr. Broome?"

"Well, I'll be leaving today, and I thought—"

"Oh, so soon?"

"Well, I finished what I had to do here, you know, so—"

"What was that, Mr. Broome? Come in, won't you, have some coffee with me."

"Well, ma'am—"

"Come in, come in," she said in a perky sort of bright cheerful voice; she was really a very nice little lady.

"Okay," he said, "but only 'cause I have to come in anyway to settle up with you."

He went into the apartment and she closed the door behind him. The apartment smelled as clean as the hallway did, with the same strong disinfectant smell. The kitchen linoleum had been scrubbed bare in spots, so that the wooden floor beneath it showed through, and even the wood in those spots had been scrubbed almost white. A clean oilcloth with a seashell pattern covered the kitchen table.

"Sit down," Mrs. Dougherty said. "How do you like your coffee?"

"Well, ma'am, I usually have it black with three sugars." He chuckled and said, "My mother says I get my sweet tooth from my father. He died in a train accident when I was only seven."

"Oh, I'm sorry to hear that," Mrs. Dougherty said, bringing a clean cup to the table and then pouring it full to the brim with coffee.

"Well, I hardly remember him."

"Here's the sugar," she said, and moved the bowl toward him. She sat at the table opposite him, picking up a piece of toast she had bitten into before answering the door. Remembering her guest, she said, "Would you like some toast?"

"No, thank you, ma'am."

"Are you sure?"

"Well . . ."

"I'll make you some," she said, and rose and went to the counter near the sink where she took a slice of bread from its waxed wrapper and put it into the toaster. "Or would you like *two* slices?" she said.

He shrugged and smiled and said, "I guess I *could* eat two, ma'am."

"A healthy appetite's nothing to be ashamed of," she

said, and put another slice of bread into the toaster. "Now," she said, and came back to the table. "You were telling me why you were here in the city."

"Oh, to sell our wares, ma'am."

"What wares?"

"We've got a woodworking shop, just a small one, you know."

"Who's we?"

"Oh, me and my brother."

"Where's that?"

"Up in Carey, do you know it?"

"I don't think so."

"It's just a small town. Huddleston is the nearest *big* town, I suppose.

"Oh, yes, Huddleston," Mrs. Dougherty said.

"There's skiing up there, if you ski."

Mrs. Dougherty laughed. "No, no, I don't ski," she said, and sipped at her coffee and then put down the cup and jumped up when she heard the toaster click. She brought the two slices of bread to the table, and moved the butter dish and the marmalade pot toward him. She sat again. As he buttered his toast, she said, "What do you make in your shop, Mr. Broome?"

"All sorts of woodenware."

"Furniture?"

"Well, not really, We make benches and end tables, stuff like that, but nothing really big. Mostly, we do salad bowls and cutting boards and wooden utensils, you know, small things. Also, my brother does some carving."

"That sounds very nice," Mrs. Dougherty said. "And you bring it into the city to sell, is that it?"

"We sell it up there, too," he said, "but not really enough to keep us going, you know. During the summer, it's not so bad because there're a lot of people up that way looking for antiques, and we get some of them stop by the shop, you know. But in the winter, it's mostly skiers up that way, and only time they'll stop in is if it's a rainy day and they can't ski. So I try to get in the city three, four times a year, mostly during the winter months." He paused. "First time I ever been here in February."

"Is that right?" she said.

"That's a fact, ma'am," he said.

"How do you like it?"

"Well, it's sure cold enough," he said, and laughed. He bit into the toast, completely relaxed, and then lifted his coffee cup and said, "Say, what time is it anyway?"

"A little bit past eight," she said.

"I guess I overslept," he said, and laughed.

He wondered if he should ask her about the police station.

"What time do you usually get up?"

"Back home? In Carey, do you mean?"

"Yes."

"Well, my mother's up and bustling around the kitchen pretty early, you know. My father used to be a railroad man, and he had an early run, so she's used to getting up early, I guess she's puttering around out there at five, five-thirty every morning. My kid brother's a light sleeper and we share a bedroom, you know, we've just got this small little house there, not much more than a shack really, so when she starts puttering around and he starts stirring, well you just might as well get up yourself, that's all," he said, and began laughing again.

"You've got a good hearty laugh," Mrs. Dougherty said. "Most big men have that kind of laugh."

"That a fact?"

"That's been my observation," she said.

He thought this might be a good time to ask her about the police station, but he didn't want to get her upset or anything, so he lifted his coffee cup and sipped at it, and smacked his lips, and then bit into the second slice of toast.

"I want to pay you for last night." he said, "I only paid you for one night in advance, you know."

"That's right," Mrs. Dougherty said. He began reaching into his pocket for his wallet, and she quickly said, "well, finish your coffee first, Mr. Broome. There's nobody chasing you for the money."

"Thank you, ma'am," he said, and smiled and took another bite of the toast.

"How old are you, Mr. Broome?" she said. "Do you mind my asking?"

"Not at all, ma'am. I'll be twenty-seven in May. May the twelfth."

"I figured about that. How old is your brother?"

"Twenty-two." He paused. "Tomorrow's Valentine's Day, you know," he said.

"Isn't anyone going to send me a valentine."

"You never can tell, Mrs. Dougherty," he said. "I'm going out to buy my mother one right this minute, soon as I leave here."

"That's very nice," Mrs. Dougherty said. She paused, and then smiled weakly, and then said, "We never had any children."

"I'm sorry to hear that, ma'am."

She nodded. He finished his coffee and then reached into his wallet and handed her a five-dollar bill. "I'll get you your change," she said.

He stood alongside the table while she went into the other room for her handbag. He decided not to ask her where the police station was. He didn't want to upset her, especially now that she seemed to be upset already about not having any children who could send her a valentine the way he was going to send his mother one. He wondered if his mother would get it in time. He supposed she would. If he bought it first thing, even before he went to the police station, and mailed it right away, he was sure she'd get it by tomorrow morning.

"Here you are, Mr. Broome," she said, and came back into the kitchen. He took the dollar bill, tucked it into his wallet, and then put on his overcoat. "When you come to the city again, I hope you'll be back for a room," she said.

"Oh, yes, ma'am, I will," he said.

"You're a fine gentleman," she said.

"Thank you, ma'am," he said, embarrassed.

"In this neighborhood . . ." she started, and then closed her mouth and shook her head.

"I'll be back later to pack," he said.

"Take your time," she said.

"Well, I have a few errands to do, actually."

"Take your time," she said again, and walked him to the door.

The drugstore was on the corner of Ainsley Avenue and North Eleventh Street. A lunch counter ran along the left-hand side of the store. The remainder of the place was given over to drugs and sundries. A rack of paperback books, their titles and covers screaming for attention, stood before a row of hot-water bottles. Beyond that, and somewhat apart from the heap of combs and syringes behind it, was a rack of greeting cards. He walked past the books – something called HOW TO DO IT ON AIRPLANES caught his eye – and directly to the greeting cards. An assorted array of birthday cards was spread out on the rack – Birthday Son, Birthday Daughter, Mother, Father, Brother, Sister, Grandfather, Grandmother, and Miscellaneous Relatives. He scanned them quickly, glanced briefly at Condolences, Anniversary, and Birth and finally came to the section devoted exclusively to valentines. More and more of the cards each year were comical. He didn't care much for that kind of card. Most of them, matter of fact, he didn't get the humor of. He looked down the row of labels at the top of the rack, and saw that these cards were classified, too, almost the way the birthday cards had been. There were cards for Sweetheart, Wife, Husband, Mother, Father; he didn't bother going down the rest of the row because what he was interested in was a card for his mother. He looked at two or three of them, and then found a nice card with a real satin heart on the front of it, and pink ribbons trailing from the heart, and the word *Mother* in delicate gold script across the top of the card. He opened it and started to read the little poem inside. Sometimes, you found a nice-looking card but the words were all wrong. You had to be careful.

He read the verse over again, and then read it a third time, pleased with the sentiment, appreciative of the way the lines scanned. He wondered how much the card cost. He liked it, but he didn't want to go spending too much for a card. He walked over to the cash register. A colored girl was sitting behind it, reading a magazine.

"How much is this card?" he asked.

"Let's see it," she said. She took the card from him, turned it over, and looked at the price on the back. "It's seventy-five cents," she said. She saw his expression, and smiled. "There are cheaper ones there, if you look."

"Well, I like this one," he said.
"It *is* a nice one."

My Mother

The joy you bring to me each day
Cannot in mere words be expressed.
The million things you do and say
Confirm you are the very best.
And even when the day is done,
And weary walk I up the stair,
Who waits for me? The only one
To smile, to greet, to love, to care —
My mother.

"Yeah, I like the poem. Most of them have terrible poems."

"It's a nice poem," the girl said, glancing at it.

"Seventy-five, huh?"

"Yes, that's what it says on the back. See?" She turned the card over and held it out to him. She had very long nails. She pointed to some letters and numerals printed on the bottom of the card. "See where it says XM-75? that means seventy-five cents."

"Why don't they just mark it seventy-five cents?" he asked.

The girl giggled. "I don't know. They want to be mysterious, I guess."

"Yes, well, XM-75 is sure mysterious," he said, and smiled, and the girl smiled back. "Well, I guess I'll take it," he said.

"Your mother'll like it," the girl said.

"I think so. I need some stamps; do you sell stamps?"

"In the machine," the girl said.

"And, oh, wait a minute . . ."

"Yes?"

"I want to get another card."

"All right," she said.

"Don't ring that up yet."

"I won't."

He went back to the rack and bypassed the Mother and Wife and Sweetheart section, searching for a section labeled Friend or Acquaintance, and finding one marked General, and then looking over the cards there until he found one that said simply, To Someone Very Nice on Valentine's Day. There wasn't any poem inside the card. All it said was Have a Happy. He took the card back to the cash register and showed it to the colored girl.

"Do you like this one?" he asked.

"Who's it for? Your girl?"

"No, I don't have a girl," he answered.

"Oh, sure, come on," she said, "big handsome fellow like you."

"Really," he said, "I don't have a girl," and realized all at once she was flirting with him.

"Who's it for?" she asked archly.

"My landlady."

The girl laughed. "You must be the only man in this entire city who's sending a card to his landlady."

"Well, I am," he said, and laughed with her.

"She must be something, your landlady."

"She's very nice."

"A blonde, I'll bet."

"Well, no."

"What then? A readhead?"

"No, no, she's—"

"Or maybe you like darker girls," she said, and looked him square in the eye.

He looked back at her and said nothing.

"*Do* you like dark girls?" she said.

"I like dark girls," he said.

"I'll just bet you do," she said, very softly.

They were both silent for a moment.

"How much do I owe you?" he asked.

"Well, let me take a look at the one for your landlady," she said, and turned the card over. "Seventy-five and . . . twenty-five is a dollar."

He reached into his wallet and handed her a bill.

"Didn't you say you wanted stamps?"

"Yes?"

"Do you have change for the machine?"

"Yes, I think so," he said.

"Machine's right over there," she said, gesturing toward it with her head. She rang up his dollar bill, and then reached for a paper bag below the counter. "Are you from the neighborhood?"

"No."

She watched him as he put his money in the machine and then pulled the lever for the stamps.

"Out of town?"

"Yes."

"Where?"

"Carey, do you know it?"

"I don't think so."

"It's near Huddleston. Do you ski?"

"Me?" the girl said, and laughed.

He licked the stamps and put one in the corner of each envelope. "Do you have a pen?" he asked.

"Sure," she said, and handed him one from alongside the cash register. "Did you ever see a colored person skiing?"

"Tell you the truth," he said, "I've never *been* skiing, so I wouldn't know."

"Oh, I'm sure there's one or two," she said. "There *must* be one or two in the whole United States, don't you think?"

"I guess there must be."

"Yeah, but I don't know any of them," she said.

"Neither do I."

She glanced at the envelope he was addressing. "Who's Dorothy Broome?" she asked.

"My mother."

"What's your name?"

"Roger Broome."

"I'm Amelia," she said.

"Hello, Amelia."

"Amelia Perez." She paused. "My father's Spanish."

"All right, Amelia," he said, and looked up at her and smiled, and then began addressing the other envelope.

"This is the one to your landlady, huh, Roger?"

"That's right."

"Mrs . . . Agnes . . . Dougherty." Amelia grinned. "Some landlady."

"She really is," Roger said.

"Mmm."

"Well," he said, and looked up and smiled. "That's that."

"Mailbox right outside," Amelia said.

"Thank you," he said. They stared at each other for a moment. "Well." He shrugged. "Well, so long."

"So long, Roger," she said behind him.

He stopped at the phone booth on the way out and opened the directory, first looking up POLICE, and then turning to the CITY OF section and finding a listing there for POLICE DEPT. His finger skipped over the various headings, Alcoholic Unit, Bomb Squad, Central Motors Repr Shop, Hrbr Precinct, Homicide Squads, Narcotic, Safety, Traffic, Youth – where were all the individual precincts? What did a man do if he simply wanted a cop? He closed the directory and walked back to the cash register. Amelia looked up.

"Hi," she said. "Did you forget something?"

"I'm supposed to meet a friend of mine outside the police station," he said, and shrugged. "Trouble is, I don't know where it is."

"Go across to the park," she said, "and start walking uptown on Grover Avenue. You can't miss it. It's got these big green globes out front."

2

The big green globes were each marked with the numerals "87." They flanked the closed brown entrance doors of the building, the building a soot-covered monotonous gray against the gray early-morning sky behind it. Roger stood across the street near the low stone wall marking the park's northern boundary on Grover Avenue, and looked at the building and wondered if anyone was inside; the doors were closed. Well, he thought, you can't expect them to leave the doors open in the middle of winter. Anyway, the police are always there, that's their job. They don't close on Saturdays, Sundays and holidays.

He looked at the building again.

It wasn't a very cheerful place sitting there across the street covered with the dirt of maybe half a century, its windows protected by wire-mesh grilles on the outside, the interior hidden by partially drawn and faded shades within. The only friendly thing about the place was the wisp of smoke that trailed up from a chimney hidden by the roof's parapets. He wondered how many policemen were inside there, and then he wondered if he should go in. Maybe it was too early to be bothering them. He walked up some fifty feet to where there was an entrance break in the low stone wall, and then walked into the park and onto the gravel path paralleling the stone wall. He looked across to the police station again, and then sat on a bench with his head partially turned so that he could watch the building.

As he watched, the front door opened, and a stream of uniformed policemen came down the steps chatting and laughing; it looked for a minute like all the cops in the city were pouring out of that door. They came down the low flat steps to the sidewalk and began walking off in different directions, some of them heading downtown and others heading uptown, some of them turning at the corner and heading north toward the river, and half a dozen of the rest crossing the street and coming directly to the wall entrance he himself had used not three, four minutes ago. Inside the park, two of them turned left and started heading up the gravel path in the opposite direction, and two of them cut across the grass and what looked like a bridle path and waved at the last two cops, who were coming right past the bench where Roger was sitting. He looked up at them as they went by, and he nodded at them briefly. One of the cops, as though he recognized Roger as somebody he greeted every morning (which was impossible since Roger had never been on this bench across from the police station in his life), sort of waved at him, and smiled, and said, "Hi, there," and then turned back to the other cop and picked up his conversation as both of them continued on the path heading downtown.

Roger watched them until they were out of sight.

He turned on the bench again and busied himself with looking at the police station across the street.

He supposed he would have to talk to a detective. That was probably the thing. You probably went in and said you wanted to talk to a detective, and they probably asked you what it was in reference to, something like a bank or a business office, he supposed.

He didn't like the idea of talking it over with somebody before they let him see a detective. That bothered him a little. He wanted to see a detective right out and clean, get it over with, instead of a lot of talk with a uniformed cop.

"That's what they are in there, all right," the voice said.

He turned, startled. He had been so absorbed with watching the building that he hadn't heard footsteps on the gravel path, and was surprised now to see a man sitting on the bench opposite him. It was still maybe quarter of nine in the morning, maybe a little earlier, and the temperature was, oh, he would guess somewhere in the twenties or even the upper teens, and the two of them were the only ones sitting in the park, facing each other on opposite benches.

"What?" he said.

"That's what they are in there, all right," the other man said.

"That's what who is in where?" he asked.

"Cops," the other man said. He was a small dapper man of about fifty, wearing a black overcoat with black velveteen collar and cuffs and wearing a gray fedora pulled rakishly over one eye. He had a small pencil-line black mustache and a black bow tie with yellow polka dots, the tie showing in the opening of his coat like the gaily painted propeller of an airplane. He gave a small meaningful contemptuous jerk of his head toward the police station across the street. "Cops," he repeated.

"That's right," Roger said.

"Yeah, *sure* that's right," the man said.

Roger looked at him, and nodded, and then dismissed him with a brief shrug and turned back to study the police station again.

"Have they got somebody in there?" the man asked.

"What?" Roger said, and turned again.

"In there."

"What do you mean?"

"Are they holding somebody?"

"I don't think I know what you mean."

"Of yours," the man said.

"Of mine?"

"In there."

"What?"

"Are they *holding some*body of *yours* in there?" the man said, impatiently.

"Oh. No. No, they're not."

"Then why are you watching the building?"

Roger shrugged.

"Look, you don't have to put on airs with me," the man said. "I've been in and out of that place more times than you can count on your fingers and toes."

"Mm?" Roger said, and was about to get up and move out of the park, when the man rose and crossed the gravel path and sat on the bench alongside him.

"They've had me in there on a lot of little things," the man said. "My name's Clyde."

"How do you do?" Roger said.

"Clyde Warren, what's yours?"

"Roger. Broome."

"Roger Broome, well, a new broom sweeps clean, eh?" Clyde said, and burst out laughing. His teeth were very white. His breath plumed vigorously from his mouth as he laughed. He lifted one hand to brush away a frozen laughter tear from the corner of his eye. His fingers were stained with nicotine. "Yessir," he said, still laughing, "a new broom sweeps clean, they've had me in there on a lot of little things, Roger, oh yes, a lot of little things."

"Well, I guess I'd better be getting along," Roger said, and again made a move to rise, but Clyde put his hand gently on his shoulder, and then removed it immediately, as though suddenly aware of Roger's size and potential power and not wishing to provoke him in any way. The sudden retreat was not wasted on Roger, who felt himself subtly flattered and hesitated on the bench a moment longer. After all, he thought, this man's been inside there, he knows what it's like inside there.

"What do they do?" he asked. "When you go in?"

"When you *go* in?" Clyde said. "When you *go* in? You mean when they *take* you in, don't you?"

"Well, I suppose so."

"They book you, if they've got anything to book you on, and then they take you back to the detention cells on the first floor there and keep you locked up until it's time to go downtown for lineup and arraignment, that's if your offense was a felony."

"What's a felony?" Roger asked.

"Death or a state prison," Clyde answered.

"What do you mean?"

"The punishment."

"Oh."

"Sure."

"Well, what sort of crimes would that be?"

"Burglary is a felony, murder is a felony, armed robbery is a felony, you get the idea?"

"Yes," Roger said, nodding.

"Indecent exposure," Clyde said, "is only a misdemeanor."

"I see."

"Yessir, only a misdemeanor," Clyde said, and grinned. His teeth were dazzlingly white. "They're false," he said, following Roger's gaze, and clicked the teeth in his mouth to prove it. Roger nodded. "Sodomy, on the other hand, is a felony," Clyde said. "You can get twenty years for sodomy."

"Is that right?" Roger said.

"Absolutely. They've never had me in there on sodomy," Clyde said.

"Well, that's good," Roger said, not knowing what sodomy was, and really not terribly interested in what they had had Clyde in there on, but only interested in what it was like once they got you inside there.

"For them to have a case of sodomy," Clyde said, "it's got to be against the other person's will, or by force, or under age, you know what I mean? They've never had me in there on that."

"Do they take your fingerprints?"

"I just told you I've never been in there on sodomy."

"I meant for anything."

"Well, sure they take your fingerprints, that's their job. Their job is to take your fingerprints and get your hands dirty and make life miserable for you whatever chance they can get. That's what being a cop means."

"Mm," Roger said, and both men fell silent. Roger glanced over his shoulder at the police station again.

"I've got a place near here," Clyde said.

"Mm," Roger said.

"Few blocks east."

"Mm."

"Nice apartment," Clyde said.

"Do they let you make a phone call?" Roger said.

"What?"

"The police."

"Oh, sure. Listen, would you like to come up?"

"Up where?" Roger said.

"My place."

"What for?"

Clyde shrugged. "I thought you might like to."

"Well, thanks a lot," Roger said, "but I've got some things to do."

"Maybe you could come up later."

"Thanks, but—"

"It's a nice place," Clyde said, and shrugged.

"Well, the thing is—"

"They've never had me in there on anything big, if that's what's bothering you."

"That's not—"

"I'd have told you if it was anything worse than a misdemeanor."

"I know, but—"

"They just think it's fun to pick me up every now and then, that's all." He made a contemptuous face, and then said, "Cops."

"Well, thank you very much," Roger said, standing, "but—"

"Will you come up later?"

"No, I don't think so."

"I have a poodle," Clyde said.

"That's—"

"His name is Shatzie, he's a nice dog, you'd like him."

"I'm sorry," Roger said.

"Please," Clyde said, and looked up at him.

Roger shook his head.

"No," he said.

He kept shaking his head.

"No," he said again, and then walked away from the bench and out of the park.

*　　*　　*

He found the post office on Culver Avenue and he went in and made out a postal money order for one hundred dollars, made payable to Dorothy Broome. The money order cost him thirty-five cents, and he spent another six cents for a stamped envelope, which he addressed to his mother on Terminal Street in Carey. He put the money order in the envelope, sealed it and then took it directly to the window and handed it to the clerk.

"Will that get there by tomorrow?" he asked.

The clerk looked at the address. "Supposed to," he said. "If you bring it in before five, it's supposed to get there by tomorrow. I can't vouch for the post office up there, though. They may let it lay around two, three days."

"No, they're very good," Roger said.

"Then it should get there tomorrow."

"Thank you." he said.

He came out of the post office and looked up at the sky, and figured there was just one more thing he had to do before going to the police station, and that was call his mother in Carey to tell her not to worry, that he wouldn't be home tonight the way he'd promised. A clock in a jeweler's window told him it still wasn't nine o'clock, but that was all right, his mother would have been up a long time already, just like he'd told Mrs. Dougherty. He wondered what Mrs. Dougherty would think when she got his valentine, he wished he could be around to see the look on her face when she opened it. Smiling he continued down the side street, looking for a phone booth. A bunch of teen-age boys and girls were standing on one of the front stoops, talking and laughing and smoking, all of them carrying schoolbooks, the girls clutching the books to their small high perfect breasts, the boys carrying them at arm's length or on straps. They'll be going to school any minute now, Roger thought, and remembered when he'd been going to school in Carey, and put the memory out of his mind, and saw the candy store some fifteen feet beyond where the kids were laughing and talking. He went into the store, saw the phone booth at the rear, and stopped at the counter to get change for a dollar bill. He waited until a fat Spanish woman came out of the booth. She smiled up at him as she went by. He sat in the booth smelling of her perfume and her sweat, and dialed the area code for Carey and then the number, Carey 7-3341, and waited while the phone rang on the other end.

"Hello?" his mother's voice said.

"Mom?"

"Roger? Is that you?"

"Yes, Mom."

"Where are you?"

"The city."

"Did you sell the stuff?"

"Yes, Mom."

"How much did you get?"

"A hundred and twenty-two dollars."

"That's more'n we figured, ain't it?" his mother said.

"It's forty-seven dollars more, Mom."

"That's right, it is," his mother said. "That's very good, son."

"It's because I went to that new place I was telling you about. The one I noticed in December, when I was in just before Christmas, do you remember?"

"Downtown there? In the Quarter?"

"That's the place. You know what he gave me for the salad bowls, Mom?"

"Which ones? The big ones?"

"Well, both."

"How much did he give you, Rog?"

"I sold him a dozen of the big ones for a dollar and a half each, Mom. That's more'n we get for them in the shop."

"I know it is. Is the man in his right mind?"

"Sure, he's going to mark them up quite a bit, Mom. I wouldn't be surprised he gets three, maybe even four dollars for those big ones."

"What about the little ones? How much did he pay for those?"

"He only took half a dozen of them."

"How much?"

"A dollar each." Roger paused. "We sell them for seventy-five at the shop, Mom."

"I know," his mother said, and laughed. "Makes me wonder if we're not selling ourselves cheap."

"Well, we don't get the crowd, you know."

"That's right," his mother said. "When are you coming home, son?"

"I sent you a money order for a hundred dollars, Mom, you look for it tomorrow, okay?"

"Okay, when are you coming home?"

"I'm not sure yet."

"What do you mean?"

"Well, there's—"

"What do you mean, you're not sure yet?"

"When I'll be home," Roger said, and the line went silent. He waited. "Mom?" he said.

"I'm here."

"How's . . . uh . . . how's Buddy?"

"He's fine."

"Mom?"

"Yes?"

"About . . . uh . . . coming home."

"Yes?"

"I don't know when."

"Yes, I heard you say that the first time."

"Well, there's something I've got to do, you see."

"What is it you have to do?" his mother asked.

"Well . . ." he said, and allowed his voice to trail into silence.

"Yes?"

"Actually," he said, "Buddy's there."

"Buddy's only a boy."

"Mom, he's twenty-two."

"That's a boy."

"I'm not much older than that myself, Mom." He paused. "I'm only twenty-seven, Mom. Not even."

"That's a man," she said.

"So I don't see—"

"That's a man," she said again.

"Anyway, I'm not sure what'll be. That's why I sent you the money order."

"Thank you," she said coldly.

"Mom?"

"What?"

"Are you sore?"

"No."

"You sound like you are."

"I'm not. My oldest son wants to leave me alone up here in the dead of winter—"

"Mom, you've got Buddy up there."

"Buddy is just a boy! Who's going to run the shop while you're gone? You know I haven't been feeling well, you know I—"

"Mom, this just can't be helped, that's all."

"*What* can't be helped?"

"This . . . thing I have to do."

"Which is what?"

"Mom, I guess if I wanted to tell you about it, I'd have done that already."

"Don't get fresh with me," she said. "You're still not too big to take down your pants and give you a good whipping."

"I'm sorry," he said.

"Now, what is it that's happened?"

"Nothing."

"Roger—"

"Nothing!" he said sharply. "I'm sorry, Mom, but it's nothing."

The line was silent again.

"You'll hear from me," he said, and before she could answer, he hung up.

3

The man huddled in the doorway of the building next to
the candy store seemed to be about Roger's age, a tall
thin man with a slight reddish-brown beard stubble. He
was wearing a gray overcoat, the collar of which was
turned up against his neck and held closed around his
throat with one hand. He wore no hat and no gloves.
His hand holding the coat collar was a deadly white.
The other hand was in his pocket. He was watching
the high school girls going up the street when Roger
came out of the candy store. As Roger went past the
building, he shifted his attention to him and came out
of the doorway and down the steps.

"Hey!" he said.

Roger stopped and waited for the man, who walked up
to him leisurely and without threat, smiling pleasantly.

"You looking for something?" the man said.

"No," Roger answered.

"I mean, you're not from the neighborhood, are you?"

"No."

"I thought maybe somebody sent you up here."

"For what?" Roger said.

"Anything you want," the man answered, falling into step as Roger began walking again. "You name it, we got it."

"There's nothing I want."

"You want a woman?"

"No, I—"

"What color? White, black, brown? Tan? Yellow even, you name it. We've got a whole streetful of women up here."

"No, I don't want a woman," Roger said.

"You prefer little girls maybe? How old? Nine, ten, eleven? Name it."

"No," Roger said.

"What then? Junk?"

"Junk?"

"Heroin, cocaine, morphine, opium, codeine, demerol, benzedrine, marijuana, phenobarb, goofballs, speedballs, you name it."

"Thanks, no," Roger said.

"What do you need then? A gun? A pad? An alibi? A fence? Name it."

"I'd like a cup of coffee," Roger said, and smiled.

"That's easy," the man said, and shrugged. "Here you meet a genie ready to give you three wishes, and all you want's a cup of coffee." He shrugged again. "Right around the corner there on the avenue," he said. "Coffee and. Best in the neighborhood."

"Good," Roger said.

"I'll join you," the man offered.

"How come everybody's so eager to join me this morning?" Roger asked.

"Who knows?" the man said, and shrugged. "Maybe

it's national brotherhood week, huh? Who knows? What's
your name?"

"Roger Broome."

"Pleased to know you, Roger," he said and relaxed
his grip on the coat collar just long enough to extend his
hand, take Roger's, and shake it briefly. The hand
returned immediately to the open collar, pulling it tight
around the throat. "I'm Ralph Stafford, pleased to know
you."

"How are you, Ralph?" Roger said.

They turned the corner now, and were walking toward
a small luncheonette in the middle of the block. A vent
blew condensing vapor out onto the sidewalk in an
enormous white billow. There was the smell of frying
food on the air, heavy and greasy. Roger hesitated
outside the door, and Ralph said, "Come on, it's good."

"Well, all right," Roger said, and they went in.

The place was small and warm, with eight or nine
stools covered in red leatherette and ranged before
a plastic-topped counter. A fat man with hardly any
hair was behind the counter, his sleeves rolled up over
muscular forearms.

"Yeah?" he said as they sat down.

"Coffee for my friend," Ralph said. "Hot chocolate
for me." He turned to Roger and lowered his voice
confidentially. "Chocolate makes my back break out in
pimples," he said, "but who gives a damn, huh? What
is it you're up here for? You're not a bull, are you?"

"What's that?" Roger asked.

"A cop."

"No."

"What then? A T-man?"

"No."

"You sure?"

"I'm sure."

"We had a guy around here two, three months ago – wait a minute, it must've been just before Christmas, that's right – he was a T-man, trying to smell out some junk. He had some case." Ralph paused. "You don't look like a fed to me, I guess I can take a chance."

"What kind of chance?"

"I mean, man, suppose you're a fed, what then?"

"What then?"

"Suppose I'm holding?"

"Holding what?"

"Some junk."

"Oh."

"It could be bad for me, you know."

"Sure," Roger said.

"I'm taking a big chance just being nice to you."

"Yes, I know." Roger said, and smiled.

"You're not, are you?"

"No."

"The Law, I mean."

"That's right."

"Good."

There was a pause as the man behind the counter brought their beverages and put them down. Ralph picked up his hot chocolate, sipped at it, and then turned to Roger again.

"What *are* you?" he said. "If not The Law?"

"Just a person. Ordinary person, that's all."

"What are you doing around here?"

"I took a room up here a few nights ago."

"What for?"

"I came to the city to take care of some business."

"What kind of business?"

"Some stuff I had to sell."

"Hot bills?"

"No."

"You're not pushing, are you?"

"What do you mean?"

"No, I guess you're not." Ralph shrugged. "What *did* you come to sell?"

"Bowls. And spoons. And benches. Things like that."

"Yeah?" Ralph said skeptically.

"That's right. We've got a little woodworking shop upstate, my brother and me."

"Oh," Ralph said. He seemed disappointed.

"So I brought the stuff in to try to sell it."

"How'd you get here?"

"In the truck. We've got a little pickup truck, my brother and me."

"What kind of truck?"

"A '59 Chevy."

"Can you carry a lot in it?"

"I guess so. Why?"

"Well, I mean how *big* a load can it carry?"

"I don't know exactly. It's not *too* big, but I suppose—"

"Could a piano fit in it?"

"I guess so. Why? Do you want to move a piano?"

"No, I'm just trying to get an idea. There are times when guys I know could use a truck, you follow?"

"For what?"

"To move stuff."

"What kind of stuff?"

"Stolen," Ralph said conversationally, and took another sip at the chocolate.

"Oh," Roger said.

"What do you think?"

"I don't think I could let you have the truck to move stolen goods."

"Mmm," Ralph said, and studied him for a moment, and then sipped at the chocolate again.

The door to the luncheonette opened. A tall heavy man wearing a brown overcoat came into the room, closed the door noisily, took off his coat, hung it on a wall hook, rubbed his hands together briskly, and came over to the counter.

"Coffee and a French cruller," he said to the counterman, and then turned to glance at Roger, and noticed Ralph sitting at the end of the counter. "Well, well," the man said, "look what crawled out from under the rocks."

Ralph looked up from his chocolate, nodded briefly, and said, "Good morning."

"I thought you hibernated from Christmas to Easter, Ralphie."

"No, only bears hibernate," Ralph said.

"I thought what you did was hole up in that apartment of yours with enough heroin to last you through the whole winter, that's what I thought you did."

"I don't know what you mean by heroin," Ralph said.

"Who's your friend here?" the man asked. "One of your junkie playmates?"

"Neither one of us are junkies," Ralph said. "You know I kicked the habit, what are you making a big fuss about?"

"Yeah, sure," the man said. He turned to the counterman. "You see this guy, Chip?" he said. "This guy is the biggest junkie in the neighborhood. He'd steal his grandmother's glass eye to hock it for a fix. Am I right, Ralphie?"

"Wrong," Ralph said. "Wrong as usual."

"Sure. How many crooked deals do you get involved in every day, I mean besides the normal criminal act of possessing narcotics."

"I'm not involved in any criminal activity," Ralph said, with dignity. "And if you care to shake me down right now, I'd be happy to have you do so. Voluntarily. If you think I'm holding."

"You hear that, Chip?" the man said to the counterman. "He wants me to shake him down. I've got half a mind to do it. When they're so eager for a shakedown, it usually means they've got something to hide."

"Argh, leave him alone, Andy," the counterman said.

"Sure, leave him alone, Andy," Ralph said.

"To *you*, pal, it's Detective Parker. And don't forget it."

"Excuse *me*, Detective Parker. Pardon me for living."

"Yeah," Parker said. "Thanks," he said to the counterman as he put down the coffee and cruller. He took a huge bite of the cruller, almost demolishing it with the single bite, and then picked up his coffee cup and took a quick noisy gulp and put the cup down on the saucer again, sloshing coffee over the sides. He belched and then turned to look at Ralph briefly, and then said to Roger, "Is he a friend of yours?"

"We just met," Ralph answered.

"Who asked *you?*" Parker said.

"We're friends," Roger said.

"What's your name?" Parker asked. He picked up the coffee and sipped at it without looking at Roger. When Roger did not answer, he turned toward him and said again, "What's your name?"

"Why do you want to know?"

"You're consorting with a known criminal. I have a right to ask you questions."

"Are you a policeman?"

"I'm a detective, and I work out of the 87th Squad, and here's my identification," Parker said. He threw his shield, pinned to a leather tab, on to the counter. "Now what's your name?"

Roger looked at the shield. "Roger Broome," he said.

"Where do you live, Roger?"

"Upstate. In Carey."

"Where's that?"

"Near Huddleston."

"Where the hell is Huddleston? I never heard of it."

Roger shrugged. "About a hundred and eighty miles from here."

"You got an address in the city?"

"Yes, I'm staying in a place about four or five blocks from—"

"The address."

"I don't know the address offhand. A woman named—"

"What street is it on?"

"Twelfth."

"And where?"

"Off Culver."

"You staying in Mrs. Dougherty's place?"

"That's right," Roger said. "Agnes Dougherty."

"What are you doing here in the city?"

"I came in to sell the woodenware my brother and I make in our shop."

"And did you sell it?"

"Yes."

"When?"

"Yesterday."

"When are you leaving the city?"

"I'm not sure."

"What are you doing with this junkie here?"

"Come on, Parker," Ralph said. "I told you we just—"

"Detective Parker."

"All right, Detective Parker, Detective Parker, all right? We just met. Why don't you leave the guy alone?"

"What is it you think I've done?" Roger asked suddenly.

"Done?" Parker said. He picked up his shield and put it back into his coat pocket, turning on the stool and looking at Roger as though seeing him for the first time. "Who said you did anything?"

"I mean, all these questions."

"Your friend here has been in jail, how many times, Ralphie? Three, four? For possession once, I remember that, and weren't you in for burglary, and—"

"Twice is all," Ralph said.

"Twice is enough," Parker said. "That's why I'm asking you questions, Roger." Parker smiled. "Why? *Did* you do something?"

"No."

"You're sure now?"

"I'm sure."

"You didn't kill anybody with a hatchet, did you?" Parker said, and laughed. "We had a guy got killed with a hatchet only last month."

"An ax," the counterman said.

"What's the difference?" Parker asked.

"There's a difference," the counterman said, and shrugged.

"To who? To the guy who got hit with it? What does he care? He's already singing with the choir up there." He laughed again, rose, walked to where he had hung his coat, and put it on. He turned to the counterman. "What do I owe you, Chip?" he asked.

"Forget it," the counterman said. "Mark it on the ice."

"Uh-uh," Parker said, shaking his head. "You think I'm a coffee-and-cruller cop? You want to buy me, you got to come higher. What do I owe you?"

The counterman shrugged. "Twenty-five," he said.

"How *much* higher?" Ralph said. "I know guys who bought you for a fin, Parker."

"Ha ha, very funny," Parker said. He put a quarter on the counter and then turned to face Ralph. "Why don't *you* try to buy me sometime, pal? Sometime when I catch you red-handed with a pile of shit in your pockets, you try to buy your way out of it, okay?"

"You can't fix narcotics, Parker, you know that."

"Yeah, worse luck for you, pal." He waved at the counterman. "So long, Chip," he said. "I'll see you."

"Take it easy, Andy."

At the door, Parker turned. He looked at Roger without a trace of a smile and said, "If I see you hanging around *too* long with our friend here, I may have to ask you some more questions, Roger."

"All right," Roger said.

"I just thought you might like to know."

"Thanks for telling me."

"Not at all," Parker said, and smiled. "Part of the service, all part of the service." He opened the door, went out into the street, and closed the door noisily behind him.

"The son of a bitch," Ralph whispered.

4

It was just the idea of going in there that he didn't like. He stood across the street from the police station, looking at the cold gray front of the building and thinking he wouldn't mind telling them all about it if only it didn't mean going in there. He supposed he could have told that detective in the luncheonette, but he hadn't liked the fellow and he had the feeling that telling this could be easy or hard depending on whether he liked the fellow he was telling it to. It seemed to him that Ralph, who was a convicted burglar and a narcotics user (according to the detective, anyway), was a much nicer person than the detective had been. If he was sure he could find somebody like Ralph inside there, he'd have no qualms at all about just crossing the street and marching right in and saying he was Roger Broome, and then telling them about it.

He supposed he would have to begin it with the girl, and end it with the girl, that would be difficult, too. Telling them about how he had met the girl. He couldn't see himself sitting opposite a stranger at a desk someplace inside there and telling them how he had met the girl, Molly was her name. Suppose they gave him a detective like that fellow Parker in the luncheonette, how could he possibly tell him about the girl, or about how they'd met or what they'd done. The more he thought about it the harder it all seemed. Walking across the street there and climbing those steps seemed very hard, and telling a detective about the girl seemed even harder, although the *real* thing, the *important* thing didn't seem too hard at all, if only he could get past the other parts that were so very difficult.

He would have to tell them first, he supposed, that he hadn't been looking for a girl at all last night, although he didn't know why that would be important to them. Still, it seemed important and he thought he should explain that first. I wasn't looking for a girl, he could say. I had just finished my supper, it was around seven o'clock at night, and I had gone back to the room and was just sitting there watching the street and thinking how lucky I'd been to have sold the salad bowls so high and to have made a new contact here in the city, that store in the Quarter.

Yes, he supposed he could tell them. He supposed he could walk in there and tell them all about it.

Last night, he had thought he should call his mother back home in Carey and tell her the good news, but then it seemed to him the happiness he was feeling was a very private sort of thing that shouldn't be shared with anybody, even if it was someone as close as his own mother, that was the trouble with Carey. That small house in Carey, and his mother's bedroom right next door, and Buddy sleeping in the same room with him, all sort of cramped together, there was hardly any time to be alone, to feel something special of your own, something private. And the room in Mrs. Dougherty's house, it was pretty much the same as being home, having to go down the hall for the toilet, and always meeting somebody or other in the hall, the room itself so small and full of noises from the street and noises from all the pipes. What Carey missed, and what the room here in the city missed, was a secret place where a person could be happy by himself, or cry by himself, or just *be* by himself.

He left the room feeling pretty good, this must have been about seven-thirty, maybe eight o'clock, but not looking for any company, instead really trying to get out of that small room and into the streets, into the larger city, so that the happiness he was feeling could have a little space to expand in, a little space to grow. He wasn't looking for a girl. He just came out of the room and down the steps and into the street – it was very cold last night, colder than today – and he pulled up his coat collar and stuck his hands in his pockets and just started walking south, not knowing where he was going, but just breathing the air into his lungs, cold and sharp and even hurting a little bit, it was that cold.

He must have gone six or seven blocks, maybe it was more, when he really began to feel the cold. It hit his feet all at once, and he felt his toes were going to fall right off if he didn't get inside someplace quick. He was not a drinking man, he didn't usually drink more than a beer or two, and he didn't much like bars, but he saw a bar up ahead and he knew if he didn't get inside someplace real quick he was going to have frostbite, well, he didn't know if he was *really* going to have frostbite, but it sure *felt* like it.

He couldn't remember the name of the bar, he supposed they would want to know its name and exactly what street it was on.

He must have come six or seven blocks, was all, walking straight south on Twelfth Street, from the rooming house. But he didn't know what avenue that would have been. He thought the bar had a green neon sign in the window. Anyway, he went in, and took a table near the radiator because his feet were so cold. That was how he happened to meet Molly. He wasn't really

No, he thought.

No, it doesn't sound right, that's the difficult part about telling it.

He could visualize it all in his head, just the way it had happened, but he knew that going into that police station and telling it to a detective it would come out all wrong, he just knew it. Sitting face to face with somebody he didn't know and telling him about how the girl had come to the table after he'd been sitting there a couple of minutes, no, he knew it wouldn't come out right, even though he could see it plain as day inside his head, just the way it had happened, her coming to the table and stopping there and looking down at him with a very peculiar annoyed look on her face, her hands on her hips.

"What's the matter?" he said.

"You've got a lot of nerve, mister," she said. "You know that, don't you?"

"What do you mean?"

"You see that pocketbook there in the corner, what do you think that pocketbook is doing there?"

"What pocket — Oh."

"Yeah, oh."

"I'm sorry. I didn't see it when I sat down."

"Yeah, well now you see it."

"And there wasn't a glass or anything on the table, so I—"

"That's 'cause I didn't order yet. I was in the powder room."

"Oh," Roger said.

She had red hair, and the red hair was the only attractive thing about her, and he suspected even that was fake. She was wearing fake eyelashes, and she had penciled fake eyebrows onto her forehead and had made her mouth more generous by running a fake line of lipstick up beyond its natural boundaries. She was wearing a white blouse and a black skirt, but her breasts under the silk blouse were very high and pointed, with that same fake look the eyelashes and the lipstick and the eyebrows had. Her hair was a bright red, almost an orange, straight from a bottle, he supposed. She was altogether a pretty sad specimen. Even her legs weren't too hot; he supposed there was nothing she could do to fake *them* up a little.

"Well, I'm sorry," he said, "I'll just take my beer and move to another booth."

"Thanks," she said, "I'd appreciate it."

She kept standing by the booth with her hands on her hips, waiting for him to pick up his bottle of beer, and his half-full glass of beer and move to another booth. The trouble was he had taken off his shoes in order to warm his feet against the radiator, which was on the wall under the table, and he had to put his shoes on now before he could move. He swung his stockinged feet out from under the table and then searched for his right shoe. He put that on while she watched him silently with her hands on her hips. Then he reached under the table for the second shoe and couldn't find it, and got down on his hands and knees and went searching for it that way. She just kept watching with her hands on her hips all the while, not saying a word until finally she said, "Oh, for Pete's sake, never *mind! I'll* move! Would you please hand me my bag?"

"I'm sorry, but—"

"Don't be so sorry, for Pete's sake, just give me my bag!"

"I took off my shoes because—"

"What *are* you, a farmer or something? What do you think this is, your own living room? Taking off your shoes? In a public place like this? Boy, you've really got some nerve, mister, I'm telling you!"

"It's just that my feet—"

"Never mind!"

"Here's your bag."

"Thank you. Thank you a *whole* hell of a lot," she said, and swiveled off angrily to a booth across the room and at an angle to the one he occupied. He watched her backside as she crossed the room, and thought some women just didn't have anything, some women were just the unlucky ones in this world, they didn't have pretty faces, nor good legs nor breasts, and even their backsides looked like a truckdriver's.

It seemed to him he always got the ugly girls.

As far back as he could remember, even when he was in the second grade at Carey Elementary, when his father was still alive, all he ever got was the ugly girls. There was Eunice McGregor, who was possibly the ugliest kid ever born to anyone in the United States, well, her mother was no prize either, that was for sure. But she had a crush on him, and she told everybody she loved him, and she warned him she would break his nose – she was a very big girl – if he didn't give her a kiss whenever she demanded one, God she was ugly. That was in the second grade. After his father died, it seemed he got the ugly girls more and more often. He couldn't understand why they were all so attracted to him. His mother had ben pretty as a picture when she was younger, and she still had a fine handsome look about her, it was the bones, you couldn't rob a pretty woman of her facial bones, they were always there, fifty, sixty, even into the seventies. His mother was only forty-six, and she still had those fine bones; sometimes she would actually laugh at some

of the girls who were attracted to him. She told him once
that she thought he was purposely looking for all the
ugly ducklings he could find. He sure as hell couldn't
understand what she'd meant by that. He hadn't said
anything to her, he didn't like to contradict her when
she said something, she'd only think he was being sassy.
But he'd thought about it a lot. It made him wonder, what
she'd said.

Looking across to where the redheaded girl was ad-
justing herself in the booth opposite, doing so with all
the fuss and annoyance of somebody who is just about
fit to bust, he felt the same happiness he had felt before
leaving the room at Mrs. Dougherty's. He watched the
girl with an odd, rising feeling of tenderness toward her,
pleased by the very fussy little annoyed female things
she was doing in the booth opposite, pulling the skirt
down over her knees, and smoothing the front of her
blouse, and tucking back a stray wisp of hair, and then
glancing around for the waiter and signaling to him in a
prissy, annoyed, very dignified, feminine way, he almost
burst out laughing. She made him feel real good. Now
that his feet were warm again (his mother had told him
never to take off his shoes when his feet were cold, just
leave them on until the feet warmed up inside, and they
wouldn't never get cold again that whole day, but he
never listened to her about his feet, they were *his* feet
and he by God knew how to make them warm) – now
that his feet were warm, and now that he had a good
glass of beer inside him and was in a nice warm place
with a juke box going at the other end with a soft dreamy
song, now he began thinking about how much money he
had got for the stuff he'd brought to the city, and
he began feeling very good about it again, and he thought
somehow the redheaded girl, well, the *fake* redhead,
had something to do with the way he was feeling.

He watched her as she ordered, and then he watched as she got up and walked to the juke box and made a selection, and then went back to the booth. Nobody in the place was paying the smallest bit of attention to her. There were maybe a dozen or so men in the bar, and only four girls besides the redhead, but nobody was making a rush to her booth, in spite of the shortage. He sat and watched her. She knew he was watching her, but she very carefully made sure she didn't look once in his direction, pretending she was still very angry because he had taken her booth.

He knew he would go to bed with her.

He wasn't at all excited by the idea because she wasn't pretty or even attractive. He just knew he would go to bed with her, that was all. He just knew that before the night ended, he would be in bed with her.

Sitting on the bench opposite the police station now, he wondered how he could explain to the police that he had known he would be going to bed with the redheaded girl. How could he explain to them that he had known he would go to bed with her but hadn't been excited by the idea, how could he explain that?

How could he go in there and tell them all about this? What would his mother think when she – well, it didn't matter, that part of it certainly didn't matter. It was just sitting across from somebody and talking about taking a girl to bed that would be very difficult. There wasn't anybody in the world he talked to about things like that, not even his mother, certainly not his mother, nor even his brother Buddy. How could he tell about Molly to a strange detective?

The idea came to him like a bolt of lightning, just like that, pow, out of the blue.

He would telephone.

He would go to a telephone booth, but wait, there were no separate listings for the precincts, how could he possibly

Parker, that was his name. The detective in the luncheonette. Parker, of the 87th Squad, and the globes across the street were each marked with an 87, which meant this was Parker's precinct. Okay, he would call police headquarters and say that he was supposed to call a detective named Parker of the 87th Squad, but he had lost the number Parker had given him, and would they please give him the number. Maybe they would connect him direct, maybe they had a big switchboard down there that connected to all the precincts in the city. Or maybe they would simply give him the number of the 87th Precinct and then he would call it himself and ask to talk to a detective – not Parker, absolutely *not* Parker – it would be as easy as that.

Pleased, he got off the bench.

He took a last look at the police station, smiled, and walked out of the park, looking for the drugstore he had been in earlier that morning.

5

The sergeant who answered the phone at police headquarters listened patiently while Roger told his invented
story about Detective Parker, and then said, "Hold on,
please." Roger waited. He assumed the sergeant was
checking to see if there really was a Detective Parker
in the 87th Squad. Or maybe the sergeant didn't give
a damn one way or the other. Maybe he received
similar calls a hundred times, a thousand times each
day. Maybe he'd been bored stiff listening to Roger's
story, and maybe he was bored stiff now as he looked
up the number of the precinct.

"Hello," the sergeant said.

"Yes?"

"That number is Frederick 7-8024."

"Frederick 7-8024, thank you," Roger said.

"Welcome," the sergeant answered, and hung up.
Roger felt in his pocket for another dime, found one,
put it in the slot, waited for a dial tone, and began
dialing.

FR 7

Quickly, he put the receiver back onto the hook.

What would he say when they answered? Hello, my name is Roger Broome, I want to tell you about this girl Molly, you see we met in a bar and

What? they would say.

Who? they would say.

What the hell is this all *about*, mister?

He sat motionless and silent for perhaps three minutes, staring at the face of the telephone. Then he felt in the return chute for his coin, leadenly lifted his hand, and deposited the dime once again. The dial tone erupted against his ear. Slowly, carefully, he began dialing.

FR 7,

8, 0,

2, 4.

He waited. The phone was ringing on the other end. He listened to it ring. The rings sounded very far away instead of just a few blocks from where he was. He began counting the rings, they must have been having a busy time over at that station house, seven, eight, nine

"87th Precinct, Sergeant Murchison."

"Uh . . . is this the police?" he asked.

"Yes, sir."

"I'd like to talk to a detective, please."

"What is this in reference to, sir?"

"I'd . . . uh . . . like to report . . . uh . . ."

"Are you reporting a crime, sir?"

He hesitated a moment, and then pulled the receiver from his ear and looked at it as though trying to make a decision. He was replacing it on the hook just as the sergeant's voice, sounding small and drowning in the black plastic, began saying again, "Are you reporting a—" click, he hung up.

No, he thought.

I am not reporting anything.

I am getting out of this city and away from all telephones because I don't want to talk to the police. Now how about that? I do not wish to discuss this matter with anyone, least of all the police, so how about that? Damn right, he thought, and opened the door of the phone booth and walked out of the booth and across the length of the drugstore. The colored girl, Amelia, was still behind the cash register. She smiled at him as he approached.

"You back again?" she asked. "I didn't see you come in."

"Yep," he said. "Bad penny."

"You mail your cards off?"

"Yep."

"Did you find your friend at the police station?"

"Nope."

"How come?"

"I figured there couldn't be no friends of mine at the police station."

"You can say that again," Amelia said, and laughed.

"What time do you quit?" he said.

"What?"

"I said what time do you quit?"

"Why?"

"I want to get out of the city."

"What do you mean, out of the city?"

"Out. Away."

"Home, you mean?"

"No, no. Not home. That's the same thing, ain't it? That's the same old box. The city's a great *big* box, and Carey's a tiny *small* box, but they're both the same thing, right?"

Amelia smiled and looked at him curiously. "I don't know," she said.

"Go take off your apron," he said slowly, "and hang it on that hook right there, you see that hook?"

"I see it."

"Hang it on that hook right there, and tell your boss you have an awful headache—"

"I don't have a headache—"

"Yes, you *do* have a headache, and you can't work any more today."

Amelia looked at him steadily. "Why?" she said.

"We're going to get out of the city."

"Where?"

"I don't know yet."

"And when we get out?"

"We'll see then. The big thing now is to do what we have to do, right? And what we have to do is get away from this city real quick."

"Are the cops after you?" she asked suddenly.

"No." Roger grinned. "Cross my heart and hope to die, the cops are definitely *not* after me. Now how about that? Are you going to get that headache and hang up that apron and come with me?"

Amelia shrugged. "I don't know."

"When *will* you know?"

"The minute you tell me what you want from me."

"*From* you? Who wants anything *from* you?"

"When you're colored, *everybody*."

"Not me," Roger said.

"No, huh?"

"No."

Amelia kept looking at him steadily. "I don't know what to make of you," she said.

"The apron," he whispered.

"Mmm."

"The hook," he said.

"Mmm."

"Headache."

"Mmm."

"Can't work."

"Mmm."

"I'll meet you outside. Five minutes. On the corner."

"Why?" she said again.

"We're gonna have fun," he said, and turned and walked away from the cash register.

She didn't come outside in five minutes, and she didn't come outside in ten minutes, and by the end of fifteen minutes he realized she wasn't going to come out at all. So he peeked over the stuff piled in the front window of the drugstore and saw Amelia at the cash register making no sign of taking off the apron or of telling the boss she had a headache, so that was that. He walked away from the drugstore, thinking it was a shame because she really was sort of pretty and also he'd never been out with a colored girl before and he thought it might be fun. Now that he had decided not to go to the police with his story, it never once entered his mind that he should go home to Carey. He had tried to explain to Amelia that Carey, and the city, and the police station sitting on the edge of the park were all one and the same thing, that it was just a matter of degree as to how you classed them one against the other. The police station was a small box, and Carey was a slightly larger box, and the city was the biggest box of all, but all of them were trying their hardest to keep a man all closed up, when all a man wanted to do every now and then was relax and enjoy himself. Which is what he thought he and Molly were going to talk about last night, when they were discussing loneliness and all. But then, of course, she had begun to talk about that man in Sacramento, instead.

He had never really had a pretty girl in his life, and Molly was plain as hell until about two o'clock in the morning, he supposed that was when it was, well, never mind that. This colored girl behind the counter was pretty to begin with, which was why she hadn't come out to meet him, he could have told her beforehand she wouldn't, none of the real pretty girls ever did. It was probably just as well. Anybody from back home spied him in the city with a colored girl on his arm, even though she was part Spanish, hell, he didn't want his mother getting wind of nothing like that. Not that he cared much about what his mother thought. If he cared about that, he'd be running right back home to Carey instead of staying here and planning to have a little fun with his time.

He wondered where he should go now that the colored girl had spoiled his plans. Actually, he hadn't had any plans even when he was hoping she'd come out to meet him. But she'd have been somebody to laugh with and talk to and show off for, and, well, he'd have come up with something, he just knew he would have. Maybe he'd have taken her to a movie with a stage show, he'd been to one the last time he'd come to the city, it was pretty good.

"Hey," the voice behind him said, "wait up!"

He recognized the voice with surprise and turned to see Amelia running to catch up with him. She was wearing a pale-blue coat with the collar pulled up high against her chin, her head covered with a vibrant-blue kerchief. She came up to him panting, vapor pluming from her mouth. Catching her breath, she said, "You sure are a fast walker."

"I didn't think you were coming."

"The boss had to arrange for relief. It took a few minutes."

"Well, I'm glad you're here," Roger said.

"I'm not sure *I* am," Amelia said, and laughed. Her

complexion was smooth and unmarked, her color a warm brown, her eyes a shade darker, her hair beneath the electric-blue kerchief a black as deep as night. When she laughed, a crooked tooth showed in the front of her mouth, and sometimes she lifted her hand self-consciously to cover the tooth, but only when she remembered. She had good legs, and she was wearing dark-blue, low-heeled pumps. She was still out of breath, but she kept up with him as he began crossing the street, and them impulsively took his arm.

"There," she said, "what the hell! If we're doing this, we might as well *do* it, huh?"

"What?"

"I mean, if I'm *with* you, I'm *with* you. So I'm with you, so I'll take your arm the same way I'd take the arm of a colored fellow I was with, right?"

"Right," Roger said.

"I've never been out with a white man before."

"Neither have I," Roger said, and burst out laughing. "With a colored girl, I mean."

"That's good," Amelia said.

"Why?"

"I don't know. I wouldn't like to think you were one of those guys who just dug, you know, *all* colored girls. That would make it a drag."

"There isn't a single colored girl in all Carey," Roger said.

"They're all married?" Amelia asked seriously, and he burst out laughing again. "What's the matter?"

"I mean there *aren't* any," Roger said. "Not a one."

"That's too bad," Amelia said. "What do you do for race riots?"

"We pick on Jews," Roger said, and realized he had made a pretty good joke, and was pleased when Amelia laughed at what he'd said. He didn't really know why there was any humor in his comment, except that the people in Carey *didn't* pick on Jews. In fact there was one Jew in all of Carey, a man named Samuel Silverstein, who ran the hardware store and who had arthritis, poor man, why would anyone want to go picking on him? He knew he never would have said anything like that to his mother or to Buddy, but somehow being with Amelia made him seem witty and daring, which was why he had made the joke. He was suddenly very glad she'd come after him.

"You always go chasing strange men in the streets?" he asked.

"Sure. You always go telling strange girls to hang up their aprons and pretend to be sick and—"

"A headache isn't sick," Roger said.

" — and meet you on street corners, and then disappear?"

"Right into thin air!" he said. "Mandrake the Magician!"

"That's what you do, huh?"

"Yeah, I'm a magician," Roger said, beaming.

"You go into drugstores and work your charms on poor little colored girls."

"*Are* you poor?" he said.

"I'm very poor."

"Really?"

"Hey, mister, you think I'd joke about being poor?" Amelia said. "What the hell is that to joke about? I'm *very* poor. I mean it. I, am, very, poor."

"I am very rich," Roger said.

"Good. I knew one day I'd meet a white millionaire who'd take me away from it all," Amelia said.

"That's me."

"Mandrake."

"Yeah," he said. "Yesterday, I made one hundred and twenty-two dollars. How about that?"

"That's a lot of money."

"Today, I've only got, oh, maybe fifteen dollars of it left."

"Easy come, easy go," Amelia said, and shrugged.

"What I did was mail a hundred to my mother."

"Up in Gulchwater, right?"

"Up in Carey."

"Oh, I thought it was called Gulchwater Basin."

"No, it's called Carey."

"I thought you said it was Gulchwater Depot."

"No, Carey."

"Alongside Huddlesworth, right?"

"Huddleston."

"Where they toboggan."

"Where they ski."

"Right, I knew I had it," Amelia said.

"Anyway," Roger said, laughing, "I sent her – my mother – I sent her a hundred, and I paid four dollars for my room, and I bought the cards and some stamps and had some coffee and paid for Ralph's hot chocolate and—"

"Ralph?"

"A fellow I met." Roger paused. "He's a drug addict."

"You meet nice people," Amelia said.

"He was," Roger said. "A nice person, I mean."

"My mother has told each and every one of us in our house," Amelia said, "that if we ever touch any of that stuff, she will personally cripple us. She means it. My mother is a very skinny woman made of iron. She would rather see us dead than on junk."

"Is it that easy to get?" Roger asked.

"If you have the money, you can get it. In this city, if you have the money, you can get anything you want."

"That's what Ralph said."

"Ralph knows. Ralph is a very wise man."

"Anyway, here's what I've got left," Roger said, and

reached into his pocket and pulled out a folded packet of bills and transferred those to his left hand, and then reached into his pocket again for his loose change. The change totaled seventy-two cents, and the bills were two fives and four singles. "Fourteen dollars and seventy-two cents," he said.

"A millionaire. Just like you said."

"Right."

"Right," she said.

"What would you like to do?"

"I don't know," she said. "Show me the city. Show me *your* city."

"My city? This ain't *my* city, Amelia."

"I mean the white man's city."

"I wouldn't know *his* city from *your* city. I'm a stranger here."

"Looking for a friend outside the police station," she said suddenly.

"Yes," he said, and watched her.

"Who you never found."

"Who I never bothered looking for."

"Bad place to look," Amelia said. "Where are you going to take me, mister? Uptown, downtown, crosstown? Where?"

"I know where," he said.

"Where?"

"There's a place I've always wanted to go. My mother brought me to the city for the first time when I was ten years old, and we were supppposed to go then, but it rained that day. Come on," he said, and took her hand.

"Where?" she said.

"Come on."

The Ferris wheels were motionless, the roller-coaster

tracks hung on wooden stilts against a forbidding February sky, devoid of hurtling cars or screaming youngsters. The boardwalk stands were sealed tight, shuttered against the wind that howled in over the ocean and raised whirling eddies of sand on the beach, leaping the iron-pipe railing and hurling itself hopelessly against the weathered boards. Last summer's newspapers fluttered into the air, yellowed and torn, flapping wildly like alien birds and then soaring over the minarets of an amusement called The Arabian Nights. The rides huddled beneath their canvas covers in seemingly expectant watchfulness, waiting for a sparrow, silent, motionless, the wind ripping at the covers and making a faint whistling sound as it caught in metal studs and struts. There were no barkers touting games of chance or skill, no vendors selling hot dogs or slices of pizza, no sound but the sound of the wind and the ocean.

The boardwalk benches were a flaking green.

An old man stood at the far end of the boardwalk, looking out over the ocean, unmoving.

"You've never been here before?" Amelia asked.

"No," Roger said.

"You picked the right time to come."

"It's kind of spooky, isn't it?" he said, and thought of Molly the night before.

"It's like standing on the edge of the world," Amelia said, and he turned to look at her curiously. "What is it?" she asked.

"I don't know. What you said. I felt that a minute ago. As if there was just the two of us standing on the edge of the world."

"The three of us."

"What? Oh, yes, the old man down there."

"He's really my *dueña*," Amelia said.

"What's that?"

"A *dueña?* That's Spanish for chaperone. In Spain, when a young girl goes out with a boy, she has to take along a *dueña,* usually an aunt or some other relative. My father told me about that. He's Spanish, you know, did I tell you?"

"Yes."

"I mean, he's not Puerto Rican," Amelia said.

"What's the difference?"

"Oh, in this city, there's a *big* difference. In this city it's pretty bad to be colored, but the worst thing you can possibly be is Puerto Rican."

"Why's that?"

"I don't know," Amelia said, and shrugged. "I guess it's more fashionable to hate Puerto Ricans now." She laughed, and Roger laughed with her. "My father's name is Juan. Juan Perez. We always kid around with him, we ask him how his Colombian coffee beans are coming along. You know, have you ever seen that television commercial? It's Juan *Val*dez, actually, but it's close enough. My father loves when we kid around with him that way. He always says his coffee beans are doing fine because he's got them under the tree that is his Spanish sun hat. He really *is* from Spain, you know, from a little town outside Madrid. Brihuega. Did you ever hear of it?"

"Brihuega Basin, do you mean?"

"No, Brihuega."

"Oh yes, Brihuega Depot."

"No, Brihuega."

"Near Huddlesworth, right?"

"Near Madrid."

"Where they fight camels."

"No, bulls."

"I knew I had it," Roger said, and Amelia laughed. "Well, now that we're here," he said, "what are we supposed to do?"

Amelia shrugged. "We could neck, I suppose."

"Is that what you want to do?"

"No, not really. It's a little too early in the day. I got to admit, though . . ."

"Yes?"

"I'm very curious about what it's like to kiss a white man."

"Me, too."

"A colored girl, you mean."

"Yes."

"Yes."

They were both silent. The wind caught at their overcoats, flattening the material against their bodies as they looked out over the water. At the far end of the boardwalk, the old man was still motionless, like a salt-sodden statue frozen into position by a sudden winter.

"Do you think the old man would mind?" Amelia asked.

"I don't think so."

"Well . . ." she said.

"Well . . ."

"Well, let's."

She turned her face up to his, and he put his arms around her and then bent and kissed her mouth. He kissed her very gently. He thought of Molly the night before and then he moved away from her and stared down at her face and she caught her breath with a short sharp sigh and then smiled mysteriously and shrugged and said, "I like it."

"Yes."

"You think the old man would mind if we did it again?"

"I don't think so," Roger said.

They kissed again. Her lips were very wet. He moved slightly away from her and looked down at her. She was staring up at him with her dark brown eyes serious and questioning.

"This is sort of crazy," she whispered.

"Yes."

"Standing here on a boardwalk with that wind howling in."

"Yes."

"Kissing," she said. Her voice was very low.

"Yes."

"And that old man watching."

"He isn't watching," Roger said.

"On the edge of the world," Amelia said. And suddenly, "I don't even know who you are."

"My name is Roger Broome."

"Yes, but *who?*"

"What would you like to know?"

"How old are you?"

"Twenty-seven."

"I'm twenty-two." She paused. "How do I know . . ." She stopped, and shook her head.

"What?"

"How do I know you're not . . . a . . ." She shrugged. "A . . . Well, you wanted to know where the police station was."

"That's right."

"To meet a friend, you said. But then you came back to the drugstore and you hadn't met this friend of yours at all, so how do I know . . . Well, how do I know you're not in some kind of trouble?"

"Do I look like somebody who's in trouble?"

"I don't know what a white man in trouble looks like. I've seen lots of colored people in trouble. If you're colored, you're *always* in trouble, from the day you're born. But I don't know the look of a white man in trouble. I don't know what his eyes look like."

"Look at my eyes."

"Yes?"

"What do you see?"

"Green. No, amber. I don't know, what color are they? Hazel?"

"Yes, hazel, like my mother's. What else do you see?"

"Flecks. Yellow, I guess."

"What else?"

"Myself. I see myself reflected, like in tiny funhouse mirrors."

"Do you see trouble?"

"Not unless *I'm* trouble," Amelia said. She paused. "*Am* I trouble?"

He thought again of Molly and immediately said, "No."

"You said that too fast."

"Don't look at me that way," he said.

"What way?"

"As if . . . you're afraid of me all at once."

"Don't be silly. Why should I be afraid of you?"

"You have no reason to—"

"I'm five feet four inches tall, and I weigh a hundred and seventeen pounds. All you are is six feet nine—"

"Six-five," Roger corrected.

"Sure, and you weigh two hundred pounds and you could break me in half just by—"

"Two hundred and ten."

" – snapping your fingers, and here we are all alone on a godforsaken boardwalk—"

"There's an old man down there."

" – in the middle of nowhere, with nothing but the ocean in front of us, and those deserted buildings behind us, so why should I be afraid? Who's afraid?"

"Right," he said, and smiled.

"Right," she agreed. "You could strangle me or drown me or beat me to death, and nobody'd know about it for the next ten years."

"If ever," Roger said.

"Mmm."

"Of course, there's always the old man down there."

"Yeah, he's some protection," Amelia said. "He's probably half-blind. I'm beginning to wonder if he's *real*, as a matter of fact. He hasn't moved since we got here."

"Do you want to go?" he asked.

"Yes," she said. And then, quickly, "But not because I'm afraid of you. Only because I'm cold."

"Where would you like to go?"

"Back to the city."

"Where?"

"Do you have a room?" she asked.

"Yes."

Amelia shrugged. "We could go there, I guess. Get out of the cold."

"Maybe," Roger said.

They turned their backs to the ocean and began walking up the boardwalk, out of the amusement park. She looped her hand through his arm, and then rested her head on his shoulder, and he thought how pretty she was, and he felt the pressure of her fingers on his arm, and he remembered again the way he had never got any of the pretty girls in his life, and here was one now, very pretty, but of course she was colored. It bothered him that she was colored. He told himself that it was a shame she was colored because she was really the first pretty girl he had ever known in his life, well, Molly had been pretty last night, but only after a while. That was the funny part of it; she hadn't started out to be pretty. This girl, this colored girl holding his arm, her head on his shoulder, this girl was pretty. She had pretty eyes and a pretty smile and good breasts and clean legs, it was too bad she was colored. It was really too bad she was colored, though her color was a very pleasant warm brown. Listen, you can't go losing your head over a colored girl, he told himself.

"Listen," he said.

"Yes."

"I think we'd better get back and maybe . . . uh . . . maybe you ought to go back to the drugstore."

"What?" she said.

"I think you ought to go back to work. For the afternoon, anyway."

"What?" she said again.

"And then I can . . . uh . . . pick you up later, maybe, after work, and . . . uh . . . maybe we can have supper together, all right?"

She stopped dead on the boardwalk with the wind tearing at the blue kerchief wrapped around her head and tied tightly under her chin. Her eyes were serious and defiant. She kept both hands gripped over the brass clasp at the top of her handbag. Her hands were motionless. She stared up at him with her brown eyes flashing and the blue kerchief flapping in the wind, her body rigid and motionless.

"What are you talking about?" she said. "I told my boss I had a headache. I can't just walk back in now and tell him—"

"We could meet later," Roger said. "For supper."

"Are you—" She stopped the words and let out her breath in exasperation, and then stared at him solemnly and angrily for several moments, and then said, "What the hell is it?"

"Nothing."

"Two minutes ago, you were kissing me as if—"

"It's just that I promised somebody—"

"Well, what scared you off, that's all I want to know. Don't you like the way I kiss?"

"I like the way you kiss."

"Well, then what? I mean, if you're afraid of being seen with a colored girl, I mean taking a colored girl up to your room—"

"It's not that."

"I mean, we can always go back to my house, where we'll be *surrounded* by colored people and also by *rats* running out of the walls, and leaky pipes, and exposed wiring, and—"

"There are rats where I'm staying, too."

"Of course, my *mother* might not like the idea of my bringing home a white man. She might actually begin singing the same old tune she's been singing ever since I was a darling little pickaninny, 'Honeychile stay away from de white man, he is only out to get in yo sweet little pants and rob you of yo maiden.'"

"Look, Amelia—"

"The only thing my mother doesn't know, made of iron though she is, is that her darling little Amelia was robbed of her 'maiden' on a rooftop the summer she was twelve years old, and it wasn't a white man who did it, or even a white *boy*. It was six members of a street gang called the Persian Lords, the biggest blackest niggers you ever saw in your life." Amelia paused. Bitterly, she said, "My *dueña* was away on vacation that summer, I guess. At the beach, don't you know? Sand Harbor, where all the society ladies spend their time, naturally. What the hell is it, Roger?"

"Nothing."

"You're not a faggot, are you?"

"A what?"

"A fairy, a pansy."

"No."

"Then why—"

"I'll meet you later, that's all," Roger said. "It's just that my friend – the one I told you about?"

"Yes?"

"I have to see him, that's all."

"He's a very convenient friend."

"I have to see him," Roger said.

Amelia sighed.

"I have to."

Amelia sighed again.

"Come on, let's go back," he said.

"I'll give you my home number," she said. "I won't go back to the drugstore, not after I told him I had a headache."

"All right."

"Will you call me?"

"Yes. Yes, I think so."

"Why do you only think so?"

"Because I . . . Amelia, please don't . . . don't push me, huh? Just don't push me."

"I'm sorry."

"I'll try to call you. We'll have supper together."

"Sure."

They barely spoke on the subway ride back. They sat side by side, and occasionally Amelia would turn to look at him, but he was busy thinking about Molly and about what he had to do. It was foolish to even imagine any other way.

He had to go to the police, that was all there was to it.

He left her off on the corner of her block. It was almost twelve noon. The wind swept through the narrow street, and she clutched her collar to her throat and ducked her head.

"Call me," she said.

"I'll try."

"I'll be waiting." She paused. In a whisper, she said, "I like the way you kiss, white man," and then she turned and went up the street and into one of the tenements.

He watched her until she was out of sight, and then began walking toward Grover Avenue and the police station.

6

It was beginning to snow.

The flakes were large and wet and they melted the moment they touched the asphalt streets, melted on the tops of parked automobiles, and on the lids of garbage cans standing alongside shining wet tenement stoops. In the park, on the stone wall bordering the edge of the park, and on the rolling ground and jutting boulders of the park itself, the snow was beginning to stick, covering only lightly and in patches, but sticking nonetheless. He walked alongside the stone wall with its pale-white, almost transparent covering of snow, and looked across at the police station and then took a deep breath and sucked in his belly and crossed the street.

He went up the steps. There were seven of them.

There were two doors. He tried the knob of the one on the left, but the door did not open. He reached for the knob directly to the right of the first one. The door opened on a very large room with grilled windows running its entire length on the left-hand side

and with a large raised wooden counter that looked
something like a judge's bench in front of the windows. A hand-lettered sign on top of the counter, bold
black on white, read ALL VISITORS MUST STOP
AT DESK. There were two uniformed policemen behind the muster desk. One of them was wearing
sergeant's stripes. The other was sitting behind a switchboard and was wearing earphones. A railing had been
constructed some four feet in front of the desk, with
lead-pipe stanchions bolted to the floor, and with a
horizontal piece of pipe forming the crossbar. An electric clock was on the wall opposite the desk. The
time was twelve-fifteen. Two wooden benches flanked
a hissing radiator on that same wall, and a small white
sign, smudged, and lettered in black with the words
DETECTIVE DIVISION, pointed to an iron-runged
staircase that led to the upper story. The walls were
painted a pale green and looked dirty.

Two men were standing in front of the muster desk,
both of them handcuffed to the pipe railing. A patrolman
stood to the side of the two men as the desk sergeant
asked them questions. Roger walked to one of the
benches opposite the muster desk, and sat.

"When did you pick them up?" the sergeant asked the
patrolman.

"As they were coming out, Sarge."

"Where was that?"

"1120 Ainsley."

"What's that? Near Twelfth? Thirteenth?"

"Thirteenth."

"What's the name of the place?"

"Abigail Frocks," the patrolman said.

"She does?" the sergeant asked, and all the men –
including the two in handcuffs – burst out laughing.
Roger didn't see what was so funny.

"It's a dress loft up there on Ainsley," the patrolman said. "I think they use it for storing stuff. Anyway, there's hardly ever anybody up there, except when they're making deliveries or pickups."

"Just a loft, huh?"

"Yeah."

"They got a store, too?"

"Yeah."

"In this precinct?"

"Yeah, it's just a little place on Culver."

"Abigail Frocks, huh?" the sergeant said, and all the men giggled again. "Okay, boys, what were you doing coming out of Abigail Frocks?" the sergeant said, and again everyone giggled.

"We was after the pigeons," one of the men said, suppressing his laughter and becoming serious all at once. He seemed to be about twenty-five years old, badly in need of a haircut, and wearing a gray suede jacket with gray ribbing at the cuffs and at the waist.

"What's your name, fella?" the sergeant asked.

"Mancuso. Edward Mancuso."

"All right, now what's this about the pigeons, Eddie?"

"We don't have to tell him nothing," the second man said. He was about the same age as Mancuso, with the same shaggy haircut, and wearing a dark-brown overcoat. His trousers seemed too long for him. "They got us in here for no reason at all. We can sue them for false arrest, in fact."

"What's *your* name?" the sergeant asked.

"Frank Di Paolo, you know what false arrest is?"

"Yeah, we know what false arrest is. What were you doing coming down the steps from that dress loft?"

"I want a lawyer," Di Paolo said.

"For what? We haven't even booked you yet."

"You got nothing to book us *on*."

"I found jimmy marks on the loft door," the patrolman said drily.

"That must've been from some other time it got knocked over," Di Paolo said. "You find any burglar's tools on us?"

"He knows all about burglar's tools," the sergeant said, and then turned to Di Paolo and said, "You know all about burglar's tools, don't you?"

"If you live in this crumby neighborhood, you learn all about *everything,*" Di Paolo said.

"Also about how to break and enter a dress loft and steal some clothes? Do you learn all about that?"

"We was after the pigeons," Mancuso said.

"What pigeons?"

"*Our* pigeons."

"In the dress loft, huh?"

"No, on the roof."

"You keep pigeons on the roof of that building?"

"No, we keep pigeons on the roof of 2335 Twelfth Street, that's where."

"What's that got to do with the dress loft?"

"Nothing," Mancuso said.

"*We* ain't got nothing to do with the loft, either," Di Paolo said. "We were only in that building because our pigeons were on the roof."

"We only went up to get them," Mancuso said.

"What's the matter?" the sergeant asked. "Don't your pigeons know how to fly?"

The patrolman laughed.

"They've got pigeons that don't know how to fly," the sergeant said, encouraged, and the patrolman laughed again.

"They know how to fly, but sometimes they don't come back when you call them. So from where we were on *our* roof, we could see these two birds sitting on the roof of the building where the *dress* loft was in—"

"Oh, you *knew* there was a dress loft in that building, huh?"

"No, we didn't know until we got over there. When we was climbing to the roof, we saw the sign for the dress loft."

"And decided to jimmy open the door while you were at it."

"What jimmy? We were going up the roof for our pigeons."

"Where are they?"

"Where's what?"

"The birds."

"They flew away when we got up there."

"I thought they didn't know how to fly."

"Who said that? *You* said that, not us."

A man came down the iron-runged steps leading into the muster room, and the men at the desk turned momentarily to look at him. He was well-dressed, clean-shaven, with eyes that slanted to give his face an almost Oriental look. He wore no hat, and his hair was a sandy brown, cut close to his head, but not in a crew cut. He was reading something, some form or other, as he crossed the room, and then he folded the form and put it in his inside jacket pocket and stopped at the desk. The sergeant looked up.

"Dave, I'm going out to lunch," the man said. "Anybody calls for me, I'll be back around one-thirty, two o'clock."

"Right, Steve," the sergeant said. "You recognize these two?" he asked.

The man called Steve looked at Mancuso and Di Paolo and then shook his head. "No," he said. "Who are they?"

"A couple of pigeon fanciers." The sergeant looked at the patrolman, and the patrolman laughed. "You don't make them, huh?"

"No."

The sergeant looked at Di Paolo and said, "You see this fellow here? He's one of the meanest cops in this precinct. Am I right, Steve?"

The man, who was obviously a plainclothes detective, smiled and said, "Sure, sure."

"I'm only telling you this because if you're smart you'll give your story to *me*, and not wait until he gets you upstairs. He's got a rubber hose up there, right, Steve?"

"*Two* rubber hoses," the detective answered. "And a lead pipe."

"There ain't no story to give," Mancuso said.

"We was going up after the pigeons, and—"

"See you, Dave," the detective said.

"—that's the truth. We spotted them on the roof from where we was flying the pigeons—"

"So long, Steve. In February?"

"What do you mean?"

"Flying your pigeons on a day you could freeze your ass off?"

"What's that got to do with . . ."

Roger stood up suddenly. The detective had gone through the door, and was heading down the front steps of the building. The desk sergeant looked up as Roger reached the door, and then – as though noticing him for the first time – asked, "Did you want something, mister?"

"No, that's all right," Roger said. He opened the door quickly. Behind him, he could hear Di Paolo patiently explaining about the pigeons again. He closed the door. He came down the front steps and looked first to his left and then to his right, and then saw the detective walking down Grover Avenue, his hands in the pockets of his gray tweed overcoat, his head ducked against the wind. Swiftly, he began following.

He could not have said what it was that had forced him to rise suddenly from that bench. Perhaps it was the way they had those two fellows trapped, the way they were trying to make out those fellows had tried to rob the dress loft when it was plain to see that all they'd really been after was their pigeons up on the roof. Perhaps it was that, or perhaps it was the way the detective had smiled when the sergeant said he was one of the meanest cops in the precinct. He had smiled and said, "Sure, sure," as if he wasn't really a mean cop at all, but simply a guy who had a job to do and the job only accidentally happened to deal with men who maybe were or maybe weren't trying to break into dress lofts.

There was something good about that detective's face, Roger couldn't say what. He only knew that there were bums in this world and there were nice guys, and this detective struck him as being a nice guy, the same way Parker in the luncheonette had struck him immediately as being a bum.

He sure walks fast, though, Roger thought.

He quickened his pace, keeping sight of the gray overcoat. The detective was tall, not as tall as Roger himself, but at least six-one or six-two, and he had very broad shoulders and a narrow waist, and he walked with the quick surefootedness of a natural athelete, even on pavements that were getting very sloppy with fallen snow. The snow was still wet and heavy, large flakes filling the air like a Christmas card, everything gray and white and sharp, with the buildings standing out in rust-red warmth. Everyone always thought of the city as being black and white, but during a snowstorm you suddenly saw the colors of the buildings, the red bricks and the green window frames and the yellows and the blues of rooms only glimpsed behind partially drawn shades. There was color in the city.

Following the detective, he began to feel pretty good again. He had always liked snow, and it was beginning to snow pretty heavy now, with the streets and sidewalks turning white, and with the snow making a funny squeaking sound under his shoes as he walked into the large swirling flakes. In Dick Tracy, whenever it snowed, the guy who drew the cartoon always made these big round white circles, they filled the whole page almost, he sure knew how to make it snow. It snowed in Dick Tracy sometimes three, four times every winter.

The detective had turned the corner into a side street, and Roger quickened his step, slipping on the sidewalk, regaining his balance, and then turning the corner and seeing the detective stop in front of a restaurant just short of the middle of the block. The detective stood with his hands in his pockets, his head bent, hatless, his brown hair covered with snowflakes and looking white from a distance. He was probably waiting for someone, Roger thought, and then looked around for a place where he could stop without attracting attention. That man up there is a detective, he reminded himself. He knows all about following people and about being followed, so make up your mind quick, do something. Either walk past him, or turn back, or find a place where you can hide, or pretend to be waiting, no, I'll go right up to him, Roger thought. I'll just go right up to him and tell him what I have to tell him, what's the sense of kidding around?

He was walking toward the detective when the taxicab pulled up, and the woman got out.

The woman was beautiful.

Roger was perhaps eight or ten feet away from her when she got out of the cab, her skirt pulling back over her knees momentarily as she slid over on the seat, her hand moving swiftly to lower the skirt as she paid the driver. The detective extended his hand to her and she took it and raised her face and her eyes to his, a rare and lovely smile coming onto her face, God she was beautiful. Her hair was black, and her eyes were a very deep brown, and she smiled up at the detective with her eyes and her mouth and her entire face, and then stood beside him on the sidewalk and kissed him briefly on the mouth, not on the cheek or the jaw, but a swift sudden kiss on the mouth. She moved away from him and took his hand, her fingers lacing into his, and they began walking toward the door of the restaurant. The snow caught in her hair at once, and she shook her head and tilted her face, grinning, and he thought at first she was one of those girls who get the cutes whenever they're around a man. But no, it was something else, he couldn't quite place what it was at first. And then, as they opened the door and walked into the restaurant, he realized that the woman was simply very very happy to *be* with this man.

Roger had never been loved that way.

He opened the restaurant door, and followed them inside.

Abruptly, he thought of the girl Molly.

7

He had walked over to her table across the bar, and she had looked up at him briefly and then gone back to her drink. She was drinking something in a small stemmed glass, a whiskey sour or something, he figured. She looked up at him with disinterest, and then turned back to her drink with disinterest, as if she were equally bored with everything and everyone in the world.

"I'm sorry I stole your table," Roger said, and smiled.

"Forget it," she told him.

He stood by the table, waiting for her to ask him to have a seat, but the girl just kept looking at the open top of her glass, where some white foam was clinging to the inside, a kind of empty despair on her face, a sadness that made her look even more plain than she actually was.

"Well," he said, "I just wanted to apologize," and he started to move away from the table, thinking she wasn't interested after all, didn't want him to sit with her. And then, all at once he realized that the girl probably wasn't used to approaches from men, didn't know how to handle a man coming to her table and flirting with her. He stopped dead in his tracks and turned to the table again, and said, "Mind if I sit down?"

"Suit yourself," the girl said.

"Thanks."

He sat.

The table was silent again.

"I don't know why you bothered asking," the girl said, looking up briefly from her drink. "I thought you just sat wherever you pleased." She lowered her eyes. Her hand came out, her fingers began toying with the stem of the cherry in her glass.

"That was really a mistake," he said. "I really didn't know anyone was sitting there."

"Mmm, yeah, well," the girl said.

"Would you like another drink?"

"Are you having one?"

"Just a beer. I don't care much for hard liquor."

"I don't, either," the girl said. "Unless it's something sweet. Like this."

"What is that, anyway?" Roger asked.

"A whiskey sour."

"That's what I thought it was." He paused. "How come a whiskey sour is sweet?"

"I ask them to go easy on the lemon."

"Oh."

"Yeah," the girl said.

"Well, *would* you like another one?"

The girl shrugged. "Sure. Why not?"

Roger signaled the waiter. When he came to the table, Roger said, "I'll have a glass of beer, and the lady would like another whiskey sour."

"Easy on the lemon," the girl said to Roger, not the waiter.

"Easy on the lemon," Roger said to the waiter.

"Right," the waiter said, and walked away.

"My name's Roger Broome," Roger said to her. "What's yours?"

"Molly Nolan."

"Irish," he said, almost to himself.

"Yes. What's Broom?"

"English, I think. Or Scotch. Or maybe both mixed," Roger said.

"*B-R-O-O-M?*"

"No, with an *E.*"

"Oh," she said, as though the *"E"* made a difference. The table was still again.

"You come here often?" Roger asked.

"First time," Molly said.

"Me, too."

"You live in the neighborhood?"

"No," Roger said. "I'm from upstate."

"I'm from Sacramento," Molly said. "California."

"No kidding?"

"That's right," she said, and smiled. She isn't even pretty when she smiles, Roger thought. Her teeth are too long for her mouth and her lower lip has marks on it from her bite.

"You're a long way from home," he said.

"Don't I know it," she answered.

The waiter came to the table with their drinks. They were silent while he put them down. When he walked away, Roger lifted his glass and extended it toward her.

"Well," he said, "here's to strangers in the city."

"Well, I'm not really a stranger," she said. "I've been here a week already." But she drank to his toast anyway.

"What brought you here?" he asked.

"I don't know." She shrugged. "Opportunity."

"Is there?"

"Not so far. I haven't been able to get a job yet."

"What kind of work are you looking for?"

"Secretarial. I went to a business school on the Coast. I take very good shorthand, and I type sixty words a minute."

"You ought to be able to get a job easy," Roger said.

"You think so?" she asked.

"Sure."

"I'm not very pretty," she said flatly.

"What?"

"I'm not very pretty," she said again. She was staring at the fresh whiskey sour, her fingers toying again with the cherry. "Men want their secretaries to be pretty." She shrugged. "That's what I've found, anyway."

"I don't see what difference it makes," Roger said.

"It makes a lot of difference."

"Well, I guess it depends on how you look at it. I don't have a secretary, but I certainly wouldn't mind hiring someone who looked like you. There's nothing wrong with your looks, Molly."

"Well, thanks," she said, and laughed in embarrassment, without really believing him.

"How'd your folks feel about you coming all the way East?" he asked.

"I don't have any folks."

"Oh, I'm sorry to hear that," he said.

"They both died when I was nineteen. My father died of cancer, and then my mother died six months afterwards. Everybody says it was of a broken heart. Do you think people can die of a broken heart?"

"I don't know," Roger said. "I suppose it's possible."

"Maybe," Molly said, and shrugged. "Anyway, I'm all alone in the world."

"You must have relatives," Roger said.

"I think my mother had a brother in Arizona, but he doesn't even know I exist."

"How come?"

"Oh, my father had an argument with him long before I was born, about a deed or something he said belonged to my mother, I don't know, something to do with land in Arizona. Anyway, my uncle hauled my father into court, and it was a big mess, and my father lost, and everybody stopped speaking to each other right then and there. I don't even know his name. My uncle's, I mean. He doesn't know mine, either."

"That's a shame," Roger said.

"Who cares? I mean, who needs relatives?"

"Well, it's nice to have a family."

"Mmm, yeah, well," Molly said.

They were silent. Roger sipped at his beer.

"Yep, I've been all alone since I was nineteen," Molly said.

"How old are you now?" he asked.

"Thirty-three," she answered unflinchingly. "Decided it was time for a change, figured I'd come East and look around for a better job. So far, I haven't found a goddamn thing."

"You'll find something," Roger assured her.

"I hope so. I'm running out of money. I was staying downtown when I got here last week, but it was costing me twenty dollars a day, so I moved a little further uptown last Friday, and even that was costing me twelve dollars a day. So yesterday I moved to a real dive, but at least I'll be able to hold out a little longer, you know? This city can kill you if you don't watch out. I mean, I left California with two hundred and fifty dollars and a suitcase full of clothes, and that was it. I figured I'd be able to land something pretty quick, but so far . . ." She shrugged. "Well, maybe tomorrow."

"Where'd you say you were staying?" Roger asked.

"The Orquidea, that's a hotel on Ainsley. There's a lot of Spanish people there, but who the hell cares, it's very inexpensive."

"How much are you paying?" Roger asked.

"Seven dollars a night. That's very inexpensive."

"It certainly is."

"It's a nice room, too. I always judge a hotel by how fast they are on room service, and whether or not they get your phone messages right. Not that I've gotten any phone messages since I checked in – after all, it was only yesterday – but I *did* order a sandwich and a glass of milk from room service last night, and they brought it right up. The service was really very good."

"That's important," Roger said. "Good service."

"Oh, sure it is," Molly said. She paused and then asked, "Where are *you* staying?"

"Oh, in a furnished room on . . . uh . . . South Twelfth, I guess it is."

"Is it nice?"

"No, no, it's pretty crumby. But it's only for a few nights. And I didn't want to spend too much money."

"When are you leaving?" she asked.

"Tomorrow, I guess. Tomorrow morning."

"Mmm," she said, and smiled weakly.

"Yep, tomorrow morning," he repeated.

"Mmm."

"How's your drink?" he asked.

"Fine, thank you."

"Not too sour, is it?"

"No, it's just right." She smiled again, lifted her glass, and sipped at it. A little foam clung to her lip, and she licked it away. "Do you like this city?" she asked.

"I don't know it too good," he said.

"Neither do I." She paused. "I don't know a soul here."

"Neither do I," he said.

"Neither do I," she said, and then realized she was repeating herself, and laughed. "I must sound like a poor little orphan child, huh? No parents, no relatives, no friends. Wow."

"Well, I'm sure you have friends back in . . . what was it . . . Sacramento?"

"Yeah, Sacramento. I had a very good friend there, Doris Pizer is her name, she's Jewish. A very nice girl, though. In fact, one of the reasons I came here was *because* of Doris. She went to Hawaii."

"Oh, yeah? Is that right?"

"Mmm," Molly said, nodding. She lifted her drink again, took a quick sip at it, put it down, and then said, "She left last month. She wanted me to go with her, but I'll tell you the truth, heat has never really appealed to me. I went down to Palm Springs once for a weekend, and I swear to God I almost dropped dead from the heat."

"Is it very hot in Hawaii?"

"Oh, sure it is." Molly nodded. "She got a job with one of the big pineapple companies. Dole, I think, who knows?" She shrugged. "I could have got a job there, too, but the heat, no thanks." She shook her head. "I figured I'd be better off here. It gets cold as hell here in the winter, I know, but anything's better than the heat. Besides, this is a pretty exciting city. Don't you think so?"

"Yes."

"It's a pretty exciting city," Molly said.

"Yes."

"You never know what's going to happen here, that's the feeling I get. I mean, who knew I was going to meet *you* tonight, for example? Did *you* know?"

"No, I didn't."

"Neither did I. That's what I mean. This is a very exciting city."

"Yes."

"So, you know," she said, picking up her drink and draining the glass this time, "when Doris left I really didn't have anything to keep me there any longer. In Sacramento, I mean. It's a nice place, and all that, but it takes me a while to make friends, and with Doris gone, I figured this was as good a time as any for me to pick up and explore the country a little myself, you know? What the hell, this is a big country. I was born in Tacoma, Washington, and then we moved to Sacramento when I was eighteen, my parents died when I was nineteen, and I was stuck in Sacramento from then on. So it was a good thing Doris went to Hawaii, if you know what I mean, because it goosed me into action." She giggled and said, "Well, I don't exactly mean goosed."

"I know what you mean," Roger said. "Would you like another drink?"

"I'll fall flat on my face."

"It's up to you," Roger said.

"No, I don't think so. Are you having another one?"

"I will, if you will."

"You're trying to get me drunk," Molly said, and winked.

"No, I don't believe in getting girls drunk," Roger said.

"I was only teasing."

"Well, I don't get girls drunk."

"No, I don't think you do," Molly said, seriously.

"I don't."

"I don't think you *have* to."

Roger ignored her meaning. "So if you want another drink," he said.

"Yes, thank you, I will have another drink," she said.

"Waiter," he called. The waiter came to the table. "Another beer, and another whiskey sour," Roger said.

"Light on the lemon," Molly said.

"Light on the lemon," Roger said to the waiter. He liked the way she told *him* what she wanted and not the waiter. Somehow, this was very flattering, and very pleasing, almost as if the waiter didn't exist at all. He watched as the waiter walked back to the bar and placed the order. He turned to Molly then and said, "How's she doing out there? Doris."

"Oh, fine. I heard from her only last week. I still haven't answered. She doesn't even know I'm here."

"What do you mean?"

"Well, I decided very suddenly, and her letter arrived the day before I left, so I didn't get a chance to answer it. I've been so busy running around trying to find a job since I got here . . ."

"She's probably wondering why you haven't written."

"It's only been a week," Molly said. "Since I'm here, is all."

"Still. If she's a good friend . . ."

"Yes, she is."

"You ought to let her know where you are."

"I will. I'll write to her when I get back to the hotel tonight." Molly smiled. "You make me feel guilty."

"I didn't mean to make you feel guilty," Roger said. "I just thought since Doris seemed to mean so much to you—"

"Yes, I understand, it's all right," Molly said, and smiled again.

The waiter brought their drinks, and left them alone once more. The crowd in the bar was thinning. No one paid them the slightest attention. They were strangers in a city as large as the universe.

"How much are you paying for *your* room?" Molly asked.

"What? Oh . . . uh . . . four dollars. A night."

"That's *really* inexpensive," Molly said.

"Yeah." He nodded. "Yeah, it is."

"Is it a nice room?"

"It's okay."

"Where's the loo? Down the hall?"

"The what?"

"The loo." She looked at his puzzled expression. "The toilet."

"Oh. Yes. Down the hall."

"That's not so bad. If it's a nice-sized room, I mean."

"It's pretty fair-sized. A nice lady runs it, I've got to tell you, though . . ."

"Yes?"

"I saw a rat there."

"Rats I can do without."

"You and me both."

"What'd you do?"

"I killed it," Roger said flatly.

"I'm even afraid of mice," Molly said. "I could never find the courage to kill a rat."

"Well, it *was* pretty horrible," Roger said. "This area's infested with them, though, you know. I wouldn't be surprised if there was more rats than people in this area."

"Please," she said, wincing. "I won't be able to sleep tonight."

"Oh, you very rarely *see* them," he said. "You might hear one of them, but you rarely see them. This one must have been an old guy, otherwise he wouldn't have been so slow. You should have been there. He got up on his hind legs when I backed him in the corner, and he—"

"Please," she said. "Don't." And shuddered.

"I'm sorry. I didn't realize—"

"That's all right." She picked up her drink and took a swallow. "I'll never be able to sleep tonight," she said, and very quickly added, "Alone."

Roger did not say anything.

"I'll be scared to death," she said, and shuddered again, and again took a swallow of her drink. "Aren't you ashamed of yourself, scaring a girl half to death?"

"I'm sorry," Roger said.

"That's all right," Molly answered, and finished her drink, and then giggled. "How large is your room?" she asked.

"Fair-sized."

"Well, how large is that?"

"I don't really know. I'm not too good on sizes."

"I'm *very* good on sizes." Molly paused and smiled tentatively, as though embarrassed by what she was about to say and do. She picked up her empty glass and tried to drain a few more drops from it, and then put it down on the table and said, very casually, "I'd like to see that room of yours. It sounds really inexpensive. If it's a good-sized room, I might move from where I am. That is, if it's really as inexpensive as you say it is."

"Yes, it's only four dollars."

"I'd like to see the room," she said, and raised her eyes from her glass for only a moment, and then lowered them again.

"I could take you there," Roger said.

"Would you?"

"Sure."

"Just for a minute. Just to see what it's like."

"Sure."

"I'd appreciate that," Molly said. Her eyes were still lowered. She was blushing furiously.

"I'll get your coat," Roger said, and stood up.

As he helped her into it, she glanced up over her shoulder and said, "How did you kill it? The rat, I mean."

"I squeezed it in my hands," Roger said.

The headwaiter was leading the detective and the woman to a table as Roger checked his coat. The woman was wearing a pale blue dress, a jumper he supposed you called it, over a long-sleeved white blouse. She smiled up at the headwaiter as he pulled out the chair for her, and then sat, and immediately put both hands across the table to cover the detective's hands as he sat opposite her. "Thank you," Roger said to the hatcheck girl, and put the ticket she handed him into his jacket pocket. The headwaiter was coming toward the front of the restaurant again. He looked French. Roger hoped this wasn't a French restaurant.

"*Bon jour, monsieur,*" the headwaiter said, and Roger thought Oh boy. "How many will you be, sir?"

"I'm alone," Roger said.

"*Oui, monsieur,* this way, please."

Roger followed the headwaiter into the restaurant. For a moment, he thought he was being led to the other end of the room, but the headwaiter was simply making a wide detour around a serving tray near one of the tables. He stopped at a table some five feet away from the detective and the woman.

"*Voilà, monsieur,*" the headwaiter said, and held out a chair.

"How about the table over there?" Roger said. "Near the wall."

"*Monsieur?*" the headwaiter said, turning, his eyebrows raised.

"That table," Roger said, and pointed to the table immediately adjacent to the detective's.

"Oui, monsieur, certainement," the headwaiter said, and shoved the chair back under the table with an air of annoyed efficiency. He led Roger to the table against the wall, turned it out at an angle so that Roger could seat himself on the cushioned bench behind it, and then moved it back to its original position. "Would *monsieur* care for a cocktail?"

"No," Roger said. "Thank you."

"Would you like to see a menu now, sir?"

"Yes," Roger said. "Yes, I would."

The headwaiter snapped his fingers. *"La carte pour monsieur,"* he said to one of the table waiters and then made a brief bow and disappeared. The table waiter brought a menu to Roger and he thanked him and opened it.

"Well, what do you think?" the detective said.

The woman did not answer. Roger, his head buried in the menu, wondered why the woman did not answer.

"I suppose so," the detective said.

Again, the woman did not answer. Roger kept looking at the menu, not wanting to seem as if he were eavesdropping.

"Well, sure, you always do," the detective said.

The funny thing, Roger thought, without looking up from the menu, was that the detective was doing all the talking. But more than that, he seemed to be holding a conversation, saying things that sounded as if they were answers to something the woman had said each time, only the woman hadn't said a single word.

"Here are the drinks," the detective said, and Roger put down his menu and looked up as a waiter in a red jacket brought what looked like two whiskey-sodas to the table. The detective picked up his glass and held it in the air and the woman clinked her glass against his, but neither of the two said a word. The woman took a short sip of her drink and then put it down. Glancing briefly at their table, Roger saw that she was wearing a wedding band and an engagement ring. The woman, then, was the detective's wife.

The detective took a long swallow of his drink, and then put the glass down. "Good," he said.

His wife nodded and said nothing. Roger turned away and picked up the menu again.

"Did Fanny finally get there?" the detective asked.

Again, there was a long pause. Roger frowned behind his menu, waiting.

"Did she give you any reason?" the detective said.

Another pause.

"What kind of excuse is that?" the detective said.

Roger put down his menu and turned.

The woman's elbows were on the table, her hands were poised in front of and a trifle below her face. Her fingers were long and slender. The nails were manicured and polished a bright red. As she moved her hands in a fluid, swift series of gestures, the nails danced like tiny flames.

For a moment, Roger didn't know what she was doing. Was she kidding, was that it?

And then he saw her face behind the hands.

Her face was more lovely than he realized, the black hair combed sleekly back from the woman's forehead, the black eyebrows arched high over deep brown eyes, no, one eyebrow was dropping now, dipping low over her left eye in a sinister frown, the woman's mouth was curling into a sneer, her nostrils were dilating, her hands moved differently now, they moved in the exaggerated slick oiliness of a silent movie villain, the woman's fingers touched her upper lip, twirled an imaginary mustache, the detective laughed, the mask of villainy dropped from her face, her eyes sparkled with humor, the white teeth flashed behind her lips, the smile broke on her face like the sound of bells, and all the while her long slender fingers moved, the detective watching her hands, and then shifting his attention to her face again, the entire face in constant motion, her mouth and her eyes augmenting the music of her hands, the sound of her hands, her face open and honest and naive, the face of a little girl, mugging, exaggerating, acting, explaining. Why, she's talking with her face and her hands! Roger thought, and suddenly realized the woman was a deaf-mute.

He turned away because he didn't want her to think he was staring at her handicap.

But the detective was laughing. His wife had apparently finished her story about Fanny, whoever *that* was, and now the detective was laughing fit to bust, sputtering and choking and damn near slapping the table top, so that Roger himself was forced to smile and even the waiter, who had padded up the table to take Roger's order, smiled with him.

"I'd just like some eggs," Roger said.

"*Oui, monsieur,* how would you like your eggs?"

"Gee, I don't know," Roger said.

"Would *monsieur* care for an omelette, perhaps?"

"Oh, yes," Roger said. "Yes, that's good. What kind of omelettes do you have?"

"Cheese, mushroom, onion, jell—"

"Mushroom," Roger said. "That sounds good. A mushroom omelette. And some coffee. *With* it, please."

"*Oui, monsieur,*" the waiter said. "Any salad?"

"No. No, thanks."

"*Oui, monsieur,*" the waiter said, and moved away from the table.

". . . began talking to Meyer at first and Meyer listened for a few minutes and then asked the priest

if he would mind telling this to me instead. I was
pretty surprised when he came over to my desk, because we don't usually get priests up there, honey –
not that it isn't a very religious place, and holy and all
that."

He grinned at his wife, and she returned the grin. God
she's beautiful, Roger thought.

"Anyway, I introduced myself, and it turns out the
pries is Italian, too, so we went through the Are *you*
Italian, too? routine for a couple of minutes, and we
traced my ancestry back to the old country, it turned
out the priest wasn't born anywhere near my parents,
but anyway he sits down at the desk and he's got a
slight dilemma, so I say, What's the dilemma, Father,
meanwhile thinking my *own* dilemma is I haven't been
inside a church since I was a kid, suppose he asks me
to say five Hail Marys?

"The priest tells me that he had a woman in the
confessional this morning, and the woman confessed to
the usual number of minor sins and then, unexpectedly,
said she had bought a gun which was in her purse at
the moment, right there in the confession box, and she
was going to take it to the shop where her husband
worked and wait for him to come out on his lunch
hour when she would shoot him dead. She was telling this to the priest because she expected to shoot
herself immediately afterwards, and she wanted the
priest's absolution in advance.

"Well, honey, the priest didn't know what to tell
her. He could see she was very upset, and that she
wouldn't sit still for a lecture on what a big sin murder was. She hadn't come there to ask the priest's
permission, you understand, all she wanted was his
forgiveness. She wanted to be blessed in advance for
knocking off her husband, and then for taking her

own life. Well, the priest took a chance and told the woman it would be nice if they prayed together a little, and then while they were praying he sneaked in a little subliminal commercial about how sinful it was to kill, Thou Shalt Not Kill, the fifth commandment, and then he explained how she was about to commit a *double* mortal sin by first putting her husband on ice and then doing a job on herself, didn't she have any children? No, the woman said.

"Well, the priest wasn't too happy to learn she was childless because children are usually a good thing to play on. So he very quickly said Haven't you got parents or brothers or sisters who'll be worrying about you, and the woman said Yes she had parents but she didn't give a damn what *they* thought and then said Forgive me, Father, because she'd just cursed in the confessional box, no less church. The priest forgave her and they continued to pray together for a little while, with the priest furiously wondering what he could do to stop this woman from polishing off hubby as he came out of his shop with his lunch box under his arm.

"That was why he'd come up to the office, hon. He told me that a priest, of course, is sworn to keep the sanctity of the confessional, which is exactly what was causing his dilemma. *Had* the woman confessed to anything, or *hadn't* she? How can a person confess to a sin that hasn't been committed yet? Was the thought the same thing as the act? If so, the world was full of thoughtful sinners. If not, then the woman hadn't done anything and her confession wasn't a confession at all. And if it *wasn't* a confession, then what sanctity was the priest protecting? If it *wasn't* a bona fide confession, then why wasn't it perfectly all right for him to go to the police and tell them all about the woman's plans?

"It's *per*fectly all right, Father, I said to him, Now what's the woman's name, and where does her husband work? Well, I couldn't get to him quite that fast. He wanted to discuss all the philosophical and metaphysical aspects of the difference between contemplated sin and committed sin, while all the while the clock on the wall was ticking away, and lunchtime was getting closer and closer, and that poor woman's husband was *also* getting closer and closer to a couple of holes in the head. I finally convinced him by saying I thought he had come to the police for the same reason the woman had gone to him, and when he said What reason was *that?* I told him I thought he wanted to be absolved. What do you mean *absolved?* he said. I told him he wanted to be absolved of possibly causing the death of two people by remaining silent when he wasn't even positive of the doctrine involved, the same way the woman wanted to be absolved. I told him I thought *both* of them wanted those deaths to be stopped and that was why the woman had gone to him, and that was why he had come to me, so what was the woman's name, and where did her husband work? This was a quarter to twelve. He finally told me, and I had a patrol car sent out to pick her up. We can't book her for anything since she hasn't committed a crime or even attempted one, and there's no such thing as suspicion of anything in this city. But we can hold her for a while until she cools off, and maybe scare her a little . . . Oh, *wait* a minute."

Roger, who was listening intently, almost turned to the detective and nodded in anticipation.

"We *have* got her on something, haven't we? Or maybe, anyway."

The woman raised her eyebrows inquisitively.

"The gun," the detective said. "If she hasn't got a permit for it, we can charge her with that. Or at least we can *scare* her with *threatening* to charge her. We'll see how it goes. Boy." He shook his head. "The thing about it, though, is I'm *still* not sure whether the priest copped out or not. Did she confess, or didn't she? It bothers me, hon. What do *you* think?"

The woman's hands began to speak again. Roger did not know what she was saying. Occasionally, he glanced at her as the wonderfully fluid fingers moved in front of her face. He had never been loved by a beautiful woman in his life – except, of course, his mother.

The waiter brought his omelette.

Silently, he ate.

Beside him, the detective and his wife finished their drinks, and then ordered lunch.

8

___

He followed the detective and his wife to a subway kiosk, where they embraced and kissed briefly, and then the woman went down the steps and the detective stood on the sidewalk for a moment or two, watching her as she descended. The detective smiled then, secretly and privately, and began walking back toward the station house. The snow was very thick now, thick in the air, falling in great loose silent flakes, and thick underfoot where it clung to the pavement and made walking difficult.

Several times on the way back to the station house, he almost approached the detective and told him the whole story. He had overheard enough during lunch to know that this was the kind of man he could trust, and yet something still held him back. As he thought about it, as he walked behind the detective and wondered for perhaps the fifth time whether he should approach him now or wait until they were back at the station house, it seemed to him the reason he felt he could trust this man was simply because of the way he'd treated his wife. There had been something very good and gentle about the way those two looked at each other and talked to each other, something that led Roger to believe this man would understand what had happened. But at the same time – and curiously, considering it was the man's wife who had caused Roger to trust him – the wife was *also* responsible for his reluctance to approach the man. Sitting alongside them, Roger had shared their conversation, become almost a part of it. He had watched the woman's face and had seen the way she looked at her husband, had watched her hands covering his, had watched the score of gentle tender things she did, the secret winks, the glances of assurance, and had been suddenly and completely lonely.

Walking behind the detective now in a silent white world, he thought of Amelia and wanted to call her.

But wait, he thought, you have to tell the detective.

They were approaching the station house now. The detective stopped at a patrol car parked outside the building, and the patrolman sitting closest to the curb rolled down the window on his side. The detective bent down and looked into the car and exchanged a few words with the cops inside, and then he laughed, and the patrolman rolled up the window again, and the detective started walking up the seven flat steps to the front doors of the precinct.

Wait, Roger thought, I have to

He hesitated on the sidewalk.

The detective had opened the door and gone inside. The door eased shut behind him. Roger stood on the pavement with the snowflakes falling fat and wet and floppy all around him, and then he nodded once, sharply, and turned and began looking for a telephone booth. The first one he found was in a combination pool room and bowling alley on the Stem. He changed a dollar bill at the desk – the proprietor made it clear he didn't like making change for the telephone – and then went to the booth and closed the door and carefully took from his wallet the folded slip of paper with Amelia's number on it.

He dialed the number and waited.

A woman answered on the fourth ring. It was not Amelia.

"Hello?" the woman said.

"Hello, could I talk to Amelia, please?" Roger said.

"Who's this?" the woman said.

"Roger."

"Roger who?"

"Roger Broome."

"I don't know any Roger Broome," the woman said.

"Amelia knows me."

"Amelia isn't here. What do you want?"

"Where is she?"

"She went downstairs to the store. What do you want?"

"She asked me to call. When will she be back?"

"Five, ten minutes," the woman said.

"Will you tell her I called?"

"I'll tell her you called," the woman said, and hung up.

Roger stood with the silent receiver to his ear for a moment, and then replaced it on the hook and went out of the booth. The man behind the desk gave him a sour look. A clock on the wall told him it was almost two o'clock. He wondered if Amelia would really be back in five or ten minutes. The woman who'd answered the phone had sounded very colored, with the kind of speech that could sometimes be mistaken for white Southerner, but more often was identified immediately as coming from a Negro. It was just his luck, he thought. The first pretty girl he'd ever met who seemed to take a real liking to him, and she had to be colored. He wondered why he was bothering to call her at all, and then decided the hell with her, and headed back for the police station.

I mean, what's the sense of this, he thought. What am I putting this off for? It's got to be done, I've got to go in there sooner or later and tell them about it, so it might as well be now. What do I get by calling Amelia, she's probably up on the roof with one of those Persian Lords she was telling me about, getting her ass screwed off, the hell with her.

The thought of Amelia in embrace with one of the Persian Lords was infuriating to him, he didn't know why. He barely knew the girl, and yet the idea of her being laid by one of those gang members, no less *all* the members of the gang, filled him with a dark rage that twitched into his huge hands hanging at his sides. He had half a mind to tell the police about *that*, too, about young punks jumping on a nice girl like Amelia, she was probably a slut anyway, letting them do that to her.

He heard voices in the park.

Through the snow, he heard the voices of children, loud and strident, cutting through the falling snow, a sound of glee, a half-remembered sound, he and his father on the small hill behind the clapboard house they'd lived in near the tracks when Buddy was still a baby, "Off you go, Roger!" and a push down the hill, the rush of wind against his face, his lips pulled back over a wide joyous grin, "That's the boy!" his father shouted behind him and above him.

There were three boys with sleds.

He walked into the park and sat on a bench some fifteen feet from where they were sliding down a wide snow-covered slope, the snow packed hard by the runners of their sleds. The boys couldn't have been older than six or seven, probably kindergarten kids who'd been let out of school early, or maybe first-graders, no older than that. Two of them were wearing old ski parkas, and the third had on a green mackinaw. The one with the mackinaw had a woolen hat pulled down over his forehead and his ears and damn near over his eyes as well. Roger wondered how he could see where he was going. The other two were hatless, their hair covered with snow. They yelled and screamed and shouted, "Watch me! Hey, watch me!" and took running starts and then threw the sleds down and leaped onto them in belly-whops and went down the hill screaming happily all the way, one of them imitating a police siren with his mouth. Roger got up off the bench and walked to the crest of the hill and waited for them to climb up again. The boys ignored him. They were talking among themselves, reliving the excitement of the ride down the hill – "Did you see the way I almost hit that tree?" – pulling the sleds behind them on their ropes, glancing back over their shoulders down the hill every now and then, anticipating the next ride down. The one with the mackinaw walked past Roger, took a deep breath and then turned to face the downhill slope again, ready for another run.

"Hi," Roger said.

The kid looked up from under the woolen hat pulled almost clear down over his eyes. He wiped a gloved hand across his running nose, mumbled, "Hi," and turned away.

"The hill looks good," Roger said.

"Mmm," the kid mumbled.

"Can I take a ride?"

"What?"

"Can I take a ride?"

"No," the kid said. He looked up at Roger in brief contempt, took his running start, threw himself onto the sled, and went down the hill again. Roger watched the sled go. He was still angry at the thought of those Persian Lords jumping Amelia, and he was also beginning to get a little apprehensive about what might await him in the police station across the way, nice detective or not. Besides, this snotnosed little kid had no right to talk to him that way. His hands began to twitch again. He waited for the boy to climb back to the top of the hill.

"Didn't your mother teach you any manners?" he asked.

The boy looked up at him from under the hat. The other two boys had stopped some three feet away, and they were staring at Roger curiously, with that odd, belligerent, somewhat frightened look all kids wear when they're expecting crap from a grownup.

"Why don't you get lost, mister?" the kid said from under his hat.

"What's the matter, Tommy?" one of the other boys called.

"This guy's some kind of nut," Tommy said, and he turned away and looked down the hill again.

"All I did was ask you if I could have a ride," Roger said.

"And I told you no."

"What's that sled made of, gold or something?" Roger asked.

"Come on, mister, don't bug me," Tommy said.

"I want a ride!" Roger said suddenly and harshly, and he reached out for the sled, grasping it near the steering mechanism at the top, and pulling it away from Tommy, who clung to it for just a moment before releasing his grip. Tommy was the first to begin yelling, and the two other kids began yelling with him, but Roger was already running, propelled at first by anger and then by a rising exhilaration as he moved toward the brow of the hill and threw the sled down and then hurled two hundred and ten pounds of muscle and bone onto it. The sled made a sound beneath his weight as though it would splinter, but it began sliding immediately and the forward motion eased the strain of the load, gravity pulling the sled down the slope, gaining momentum, two hundred and ten pounds hurtling down the hill, faster, faster, he opened his mouth and yelled like a kid, "Wheeeeeeeeeeeeeee!" as the sled raced through the falling snow. Behind him, Tommy and the other kids were shouting and ranting and running down the hill after him, he didn't give a damn about them. His eyes were tearing from the wind roaring over the front end of the sled, the big falling flakes made visibility almost impossible, the sled suddenly turned over and he rolled into the snow, the sled flying up into the air, he landing on his side and continuing to roll down the hill, laughing as his coat and his trousers and his face and his hair got covered with snow, and then finally sitting up at the base of the hill, still laughing, and looking up to where Tommy and the others were yelling as they retrieved the sled from a snowbank.

"Call a cop, Tommy," one of the boys said.

"Go on, do it," the other boy said.

Roger got to his feet. Laughing, he glanced over his shoulder once, quickly, and began running.

He wondered how much time had passed. Was it five or ten minutes already, would Amelia be back?

He laughed again. That ride had really been something, he'd left those little yelling bastards clear up at the top of the hill, boy that had really been something. He shook his head in bemused wonder and then suddenly stopped and threw back his head and shouted "Yahoooo!" to the falling snowflakes, and then began running again, out of the park. He stopped running when he reached the sidewalk. He put his hands into his coat pockets and began walking at a very gentlemanly dignified pace. He could remember him and his father and the fun they used to have together before Buddy was born, and even when Buddy was just a little baby. And then of course when Buddy was two, his father had got killed, and it was Roger who'd had to take care of the family, that was what his mother had told him at the time, even though he was only seven years old, It's you who's the man in the family now, Roger. Riding down the hill on that kid's sled had been just like it was before his father died, just a lot of fun, that was all. And now, walking like a gentleman on the sidewalk, this was the way it got *after* his father was killed in the train wreck, you couldn't kid around too much anymore, you had to be a man. It's you who's the man in the family now, Roger.

Seven years old, he thought.

How the hell can you be a man at seven?

Well, I was always big for my age.

Still.

He shrugged.

He was beginning to feel depressed, he didn't know why. His face was wet with snow, and he wiped one hand over it, and then reached into his pocket for a handkerchief, and wiped his face again. He guessed he should try Amelia. He guessed he should go talk to that detective.

He began making bargains with himself. If the next car that comes down the street is a black Chevrolet, then I'll go to the police station and talk to the detective. But if the next car that comes down is a taxicab, I'll call Amelia. If it's a truck, though, I'll go back to my room and pack my bag and just go home, probably be best anyway, people worrying about me back home. No cars were coming down the street for a while because the snow was so thick, and when one finally did pass, it was a blue Ford convertible, for which he had made no provisions. He said the hell with it and found a phone booth and dialed Amelia's number.

The same woman answered the phone.

"What do you want?" she said.

"This is Roger Broome again," he said. "I want to talk to Amelia."

"Just a minute," the woman said, and then she partially covered the mouthpiece and Roger heard her shout, "'Melia! It's your Mr. Charlie!"

Roger waited.

When Amelia came to the phone, he said immediately, "Who's Mr. Charlie?"

"I'll tell you later. Where are you?"

"I don't know, somewhere near the park."

"Did you want to see me?" Amelia asked.

"Yes."

"I can't come down for a while. I'm helping my mother with the curtains."

"Was that your mother who answered the phone?"

"Yes."

"She sounds very sweet."

"Yes, she's a charmer," Amelia said.

"What did you say you were helping her with?"

"The curtains. She made some new curtains, and we were putting them up."

"Can't she do that alone?"

"No." Amelia paused. "I'll meet you later, if you like."

"All right. When later?"

"An hour?"

"All right. Where?"

"Oh, gee, I don't know. How about the drugstore?"

"Okay, the drugstore," Roger said. "What time is it now?"

"It's about two-twenty, I guess. Let's say three-thirty, to be sure."

"Okay, the drugstore at three-thirty," Roger said.

"Yes. You know where it is, don't you?"

"Sure I do. Where is it?"

Amelia laughed. "On the corner of Ainsley and North Eleventh."

"Ainsley and North Eleventh, right," Roger said.

"Three-thirty."

"Three-thirty, right." Roger paused. "Who's Mr. Charlie?"

"*You're* Mr. Charlie."

"I am?"

Amelia laughed again. "I'll tell you all about it when I see you. I'll give you a course in black-white relations."

"Oh, boy," Roger said.

"And other things," Amelia whispered.

"Okay," Roger said. His heart was pounding. "Three-thirty at the drugstore. I'll go home and put on a clean shirt."

"Okay."

"So long," he said.

"So long," she said.

A squad car was parked at the curb when he got back to the rooming house.

The car was empty. The window near the curb was lowered, and he could hear the police radio going inside. He looked up the steps leading to the front door. Through the glass panels on the door he could see Mrs. Dougherty in conversation with two uniformed policemen.

He was about to turn and walk off in the opposite direction when one of the cops looked through the glass-paneled door directly at him. He couldn't turn and walk away now that he'd been seen, so he walked casually up the steps and kicked snow from his feet on the top step and then opened the door and walked into the vestibule. A radiator was hissing behind the fat cop, who stood with his hands behind his back, the fingers spread toward the heat. Mrs. Dougherty was explaining something to the cops as Roger stepped into the vestibule. ". . . only discovered it half an hour ago when I went down to the basement to put in some laundry, so that was when I called you, hello, Mr. Broome."

"Hello, Mrs. Dougherty," he said. "Is something wrong?"

"Oh, nothing important," she said, and turned back to the policemen as he went past. "It's not that it was new or anything," she said to the fat cop. Roger opened the inner vestibule door. "But I suppose it was worth maybe fifty or sixty dollars, I don't know. What annoys me is that somebody could get into the basement and . . ."

Roger closed the door and went up the steps to his room.

He had just taken off his coat when the knock sounded on his door.

"Who is it?" he said.

"Me. Fook."

"Who?"

"Fook. Fook Shanahan. Open up."

Roger went to the door and unlocked it. Fook was a small, bald, bright-eyed man of about forty-five, wearing a white shirt over which was an open brown cardigan sweater. He was grinning as Roger opened the door, and he stepped into the room with an air of conspiracy, and immediately closed and locked the door behind him.

"Did you see the cops downstairs?" he asked at once.

"Yes," Roger said.

"Something, huh?" Fook said, his eyes gleaming.

"What do they want?"

"Don't you know what happened?"

"No. What?"

"Somebody robbed the bloodsucker."

"Who do you mean?"

"Dougherty, Dougherty, our landlady, who do you think I mean?"

"She's a nice lady," Roger said.

"Oh boy oh boy oh boy oh boy," Fook said. "A nice lady, oh boy oh boy."

"She seems like a nice lady to me," Roger said.

"That's because you've only been here a few days," Fook said. "I've been living in this dump for six years now, *six* years, and I'm telling you she's a bloodsucker and a tightwad and the meanest old bitch who ever walked the earth, that's what I'm telling you."

"Well," Roger said, and shrugged.

"I'm glad they robbed the old bitch."

"What'd they take?"

"Not enough," Fook said. "You got a drink in here?"

"What? No, I'm sorry."

"I'll be right back."

"Where are you going?"

"My room. I've got a bottle in there. Have you got some glasses?"

"Just the one on the sink there."

"I'll bring my own," Fook said, and went out.

Well, Roger thought, I suppose she had to find out it was missing sooner or later. It was just that I didn't expect her to find out so soon. Or maybe I didn't expect her to call the police even if she *did* find out. But she did and she has, and they're downstairs now, so maybe this is as good a time as any to get drunk with

Fook. No, I'm supposed to meet Amelia at three-thirty.

I should have been more careful.

Still, at the time, it seemed like the right thing to do. Maybe it was.

A knock sounded on the door.

"Come in," he said.

It was Fook. He came in carrying a partially filled bottle of bourbon with a water glass turned upside down over the neck of the bottle. He put the bottle down on the dresser and then walked quickly to the sink, where he picked up Roger's glass. He went back to the dresser, put Roger's glass down, lifted the upturned glass from the neck of the bottle, put that one down beside the other and then lifted the bottle.

"Say when," he said.

"I'm not a drinker," Roger said.

"Neither am I," Fook said, and winked and poured half a tumblerful of whiskey.

"That's too much for me," Roger said.

"All right, I'll have this one," Fook said, and began pouring into the other glass.

"That's enough," Roger said.

"Have a little more. We're celebrating."

"What are we celebrating?"

Fook poured another finger of whiskey into Roger's glass and then carried it to him. He extended his own glass and said, "Here's to Mrs. Dougherty's loss, may the old bitch be uncovered."

"Uncovered?"

"By insurance." Fook winked, raised his glass to his lips, and took a healthy swallow of the bourbon. "Also, may this be only the first of a long line of losses to come. May some no-good thief sneak into the lady's basement *tomorrow* night and steal perhaps her washtub, and the *next* night her oil burner, and the *next* night her underwear hanging on a line down there. May all the crooks in this crumby city come to Mrs. Dougherty's basement night after night and pick it clean like a bunch of vultures going over her bones. May loss pile upon loss until the old bitch has nothing left but the clothes on her back, and then may some bold rapist climb through her window one night and do a job on the scrawny wretch, leaving her nary a nightgown to keep her warm. Amen," Fook said, and drained his glass. He poured it full again, almost to the brim. "You're not drinking, my friend," he said.

"I'm drinking," Roger answered, and sipped at the bourbon.

"An icebox," Fook said.

Roger said nothing.

"It strikes me as amusing that anybody would come into Mrs. Dougherty's basement and steal an icebox, I beg your pardon, a *refrig*erator, that has been sitting there for God knows how long gathering dust. It raises a great many questions which to me are both amusing *and* amazing," Fook said.

"Like what?"

"Like number one, how would anyone *know* the old bitch had an icebox, I beg your pardon a *refrig*erator, in the basement? How many times have you been in the basement of this building?"

"I've never been in the basement," Roger said.

"Exactly. I've lived in this crumby dump for six full years, and I've been down there only twice, once to put an old trunk of mine on a shelf and another time when Mother Dougherty fainted at the sight of a rat down there and screamed loud enough to wake the whole building, me included, who went down there to find the scrawny witch spreadeagled on the floor unconscious with her dress up round her skinny ass, a sight to make a man puke, have another drink."

"I haven't finished this one yet."

"So how would anyone know there was a refrigerator down there, that's number one. And if he *did* know about the refrigerator, then he also knew it was a vintage appliance, circa 1939 or '40, and worth perhaps ten dollars, if not less. Why would a man go to the trouble of stealing a decrepit wreck like that? Why, *lifting* the thing alone would be enough to give a man a hernia." Fook poured another drink and then said, "I'm talking about a normal man like myself. A man *your* size could lift it without batting an eyelash."

"Well, I don't know," Roger said, and shrugged.

"In any case," Fook said, "how would anyone *know* it was down there, number one – and number two, why would anyone *want* to steal a piece of garbage worth at most five or six dollars?"

"Maybe he had some need for it," Roger suggested.

"Like what?"

"I don't know," Roger said.

"What, why*ever* he did it, I'm glad he did it. I only wish he'd taken more while he was at it. Isn't it just like that old bitch, though, to go screaming to the cops immediately over a piece of junk like that old refrigerator? She's tying up the whole damn police force over a machine that was worth three or four bucks."

"Well, there were only two cops down there," Roger said.

"Those are the beat cops," Fook said. "In a burglary, they always precede the bulls. You wait and see. The bulls'll be here today asking questions and snooping around, wasting the taxpayers' time and money, and all for a lousy refrigerator that wouldn't bring two and a half bucks on the open market, have another drink."

"Thanks," Roger said, and extended his glass.

9

The knock on the door awakened him.

Fook had left at about a quarter to three, taking the remainder of the bourbon with him. Roger had drunk only the two drinks, but he wasn't used to hard whiskey, and he must have begun dozing shortly afterward. He wondered what time it was now. He couldn't have been asleep too long. He sat up in bed and looked around the room, dazed, and then blinked as the knock sounded again.

"Who is it?" he asked.

"Police," the voice answered.

Police, he thought.

"Just a moment," he said.

It was probably about the refrigerator. Fook had said detectives would come around asking about the refrigerator. He swung his legs over the side of the bed and went to the door. It was unlocked. He twisted the knob and opened the door wide.

Two men were standing in the hallway. One was very tall, and the other was short. The tall one had red hair with a jagged white streak across the right temple.

"Mr. Broome?" the short one said.

"Yes?" Roger answered.

"I'm Detective Willis," the short one said. "This is my partner, Detective Horse. We wonder if we could ask you a few questions."

"Sure, come in," Roger said.

He moved back and away from the door. Willis entered the room first and then Horse – had he said *Horse?* – came in after him and closed the door. Roger sat on the edge of the bed and then indicated the two chairs in the room and said, "Have a seat, won't you?"

Willis sat in the hard-backed chair near the dresser. Horse – his name *couldn't* be Horse – stood just behind the chair, one hand resting on the dresser. They were both wearing heavy overcoats. Willis kept his buttoned. The other one had opened his; he was wearing a plaid sports jacket. Roger could see a leather gun holster clipped to his waist in the opening of the coat and jacket.

"I'm sorry,"' he said, "*what* did you say your name was?"

"Me?"

"Yes. Um-huh."

"Hawes."

Roger nodded.

"H-A-W-E-S," the detective said.

"Oh." Roger smiled. "I thought you said Horse."

"No."

"That would be a funny name. Horse, I mean."

"No, it's Hawes."

"Sure," Roger said.

The room went silent.

"Mr. Broome," Willis said, "we got a list of all the tenants from your landlady, Mrs. Dougherty, and we're just making a routine check through the building. I guess you know a refrigerator was stolen from the basement sometime last night."

"Yes," he said.

"How did you hear about it, Mr. Broome?" Hawes asked.

"Fook told me. Fook Shanahan. He has a room down the hall."

"Fook?" Hawes said.

"I think his real name is Frank Hubert Shanahan, or something like that. Fook is a nickname."

"I see," Hawes said. "When did he tell you about it, Mr. Broome?"

"Oh, I don't know. What time is it now?"

Willis looked at his watch. "Three o'clock."

"About a half-hour ago, I guess. Or maybe fifteen minutes, I don't know. He stopped in to tell me about it, and we had a few drinks."

"But you hadn't known about the refrigerator until he told you, is that right?"

"That's right. Well, actually, I knew something was wrong when I got home a little while ago because I saw Mrs. Dougherty downstairs talking to two policemen."

"But you didn't know exactly *what* was wrong until Mr. Shanahan told you about the refrigerator."

"That's right."

The two detectives looked at him and said nothing. It almost seemed for a moment that they had no further questions. Willis cleared his throat.

"You understand, Mr. Broome," he said, "that this is all routine, and we're in no way implying—"

"Oh, sure," Roger said.

"The logical place to start an investigation, though, is with the tenants of a building, those who would have had access—"

"Oh, sure," Roger said.

"—to the item or items stolen."

"Sure."

The room went silent again.

"Mr. Broome, I wonder if you could tell us where you were last night."

"What time last night?"

"Well, let's start with dinner. Where did you have dinner?"

"Gee, I don't remember," Roger said. "Someplace around here, a little Italian restaurant." He paused. "I'm not too familiar with the city, you see. I don't get in too often. I've only been here a few days this trip."

"Doing what, Mr. Broome?"

"Selling woodenware."

"What's that, Mr. Broome? What kind of woodenware?"

"We've got a little shop up home, we make coffee tables and bowls, spoons, things like that. We sell the stuff to places in the city. That's why I'm here."

"When do you plan to go home?"

"I really should be getting back tonight." Roger shrugged. "I sold all the stuff yesterday. I've really got no reason to hang around."

"Where is that, Mr. Broome? Your home."

"Carey." He paused. "It's near Huddleston," he said automatically.

"Oh, yes," Hawes said.

"You know it?"

"I've skied Mount Torrance," Hawes said.

"You have?"

"Yes. Nice area up there."

"Well, our shop is on 190, just east of Huddleston. The turnoff just before the mountain road."

"Oh, yes," Hawes said.

"How about that?" Roger said, and he smiled. "Small world."

"It sure is," Hawes said, and returned the smile.

"What time would you say you had dinner, Mr. Broome?" Willis asked.

"Must've been about five."

"So early?"

"Well, we eat early back home, I guess I'm used to it." He shrugged.

"What'd you do after dinner?"

"Came back here."

"What time was that?"

"Six-thirty? Around then."

"Did you stay in after that?"

"No."

"Where'd you go?"

"To a bar."

"Where?"

"Right in the neighborhood, oh, no more'n six or seven blocks from here, walking south on Twelfth Street."

"Would you remember the name of the bar?"

"No, I'm sorry. I really went out for a walk. I only stopped in the bar because I was getting kind of chilly. I'm not usually a drinking man."

"But you did have a drink with Mr. Shanahan just a little while ago, didn't you?" Hawes asked.

"Oh, yeah, *that*," Roger said, and laughed. "We were celebrating."

"Celebrating what?"

"Well, I shouldn't even tell you this, you'll get the wrong idea."

"What's that?" Hawes said, smiling.

"Well, Fook doesn't care too much for Mrs. Dougherty, you know. He was glad somebody stole her old refrigerator." Roger laughed again. "So he wanted to have a few drinks to celebrate."

"You don't think *he* stole it, do you?" Willis said.

"Who? Fook? No." Roger shook his head. "Oh, no, he wouldn't do anything like that. He was just glad it happened, that's all. No. Listen, I don't mean to get Fook in trouble by what I said. He's a very nice person. He's not a thief, I can tell you that."

"Mm-huh," Willis said. "What time did you leave the bar, Mr. Broome?"

"Midnight? I don't know. About then."

"Do you have a watch?"

"No."

"Then you're not sure it was midnight."

"It must've been around then. I was pretty sleepy. I usually get pretty sleepy around that time."

"Were you alone?" Hawes asked.

"Yes," Roger said, and looked at the detectives squarely and wondered if they could tell he had just lied to them for the first time.

"What'd you do when you left the bar?"

"Came back here," Roger said. That was true, anyway. He *had* come back to the room.

"And then what?"

"I went to bed." That was true, too.

"Did you go right to sleep?"

"Well, not right off." He was still telling the truth. More or less.

"When *did* you fall asleep?" Hawes asked.

"Oh, I don't really remember. A half-hour, an hour. It's hard to tell just when you drop off, you know."

"Mmm," Willis said, "it is. Did you hear anything strange while you were in bed trying to fall asleep?"

"What do you mean, strange?"

"Any strange noises."

"Well, what kind of noises?"

"Anything out of the ordinary," Hawes said.

"No, I didn't hear anything."

"Anything wake you during the night?"

"No."

"You didn't hear any noises in the street outside, you know, maybe men's voices, or the sound of someone struggling with a heavy load, anything like that?"

"No, I didn't."

"Or something being dragged or pulled?"

"No. This is the third floor," Roger said. "Be pretty hard to hear anything like that, even if I wasn't asleep." He paused. "I'm a pretty sound sleeper." He paused again. "Excuse me, but would you know what time it is?"

Willis looked at his watch. "Three-ten," he said.

"Thank you."

"Do you have an appointment, Mr. Broome?"

"Yeah, I'm supposed to meet somebody."

"What do you suppose that refrigerator was worth?" Hawes asked suddenly.

"I don't know," Roger said. "I never saw it."

"Have you ever been down in the basement of this building?"

"No," Roger said.

"Mrs. Dougherty says it was worth about fifty dollars," Willis said. "Do you agree with her?"

"I never saw it," Roger said, "so I couldn't say. Fook says it wasn't worth more than a few dollars."

"The only reason we bring up the value," Willis said, "is that it would make a difference in the charge."

"The charge?"

"Yes, the criminal charge. If the value was under twenty-five dollars, it would be petit larceny. That's only a misdemeanor."

"I see," Roger said.

"If the crime's committed at night, and the property is taken from the *person* of another," Willis went on, "that's automatically grand larceny. But if it was taken from a dwelling place . . ." Willis paused. "Somebody's house, you know?"

"Yes?"

"Yes, and at *night* also, then the value has to be more than twenty-five dollars for it to be grand larceny."

"Oh," Roger said.

"Yeah. Grand larceny's a felony, you know. You can get up to ten years on a grand larceny conviction."

"Is that right?" Roger said. "For a measly twenty-five dollars? Boy!" He shook his head.

"Oh, sure," Willis said. He looked at Hawes. "You got any questions, Cotton?"

"Are those the only windows?" Hawes asked.

"Those?" Roger said. "Yes, they're the only ones."

"You don't have any facing on the back yard?"

"No."

"I just can't see anybody hauling that heavy refrigerator all the way out to the front of the building," Hawes said. "A car or a truck must have backed into the alley to the basement door. That's what I think." He shrugged. "Well, Mr. Broome wouldn't have heard it, anyway. His windows face the front."

"That's right," Roger said.

Willis sighed. "You've been very cooperative, Mr. Brome. Thank you very much."

"I hope we haven't kept you from your appointment," Hawes said.

"No, I'm supposed to meet her at three-thirty," Roger said.

"Thanks again," Willis said.

"Glad to help," Roger said. He walked them to the door. "Will you be needing anything else from me?"

"No, I don't think so," Hawes said. He turned to Willis. "Hal?"

"I don't think so, Mr. Broome. I hope you understand

we *had* to make a routine check of all the—"

"Oh, sure," Roger said.

"Chances are this was a neighborhood junkie," Hawes said.

"Or a kid. Sometimes it's kids," Willis said.

"We get a lot of little thefts," Hawes said. "Not much we can do about them unless we're lucky enough to turn up a witness."

"Or sometimes we'll catch some guy, oh, maybe six months from now – on something else, you understand – and he'll tell us all about having swiped a refrigerator from a basement back in February. That's the way it goes." Willis smiled. "We try to keep up with it."

"Well, I wish you luck," Roger said. He opened the door.

"As far as you're concerned though," Hawes said, "you can forget all about it. Go home, stay a few days, entirely up to you. We won't be bothering you any further."

"Well, thank you," Roger said.

"Thank *you* for your time, sir," Hawes said.

"Thank you," Willis said.

They both went out. Roger closed the door behind them. He waited until he could no longer hear their footsteps, and then he locked the door.

Molly's scarf was in the bottom drawer of his dresser.

10

They had come back to the room at a little past midnight, coming quietly up the steps to the third floor, walking past Fook's apartment, and then pausing silently outside Roger's room as he searched for his key and unlocked the door. They stepped inside, and he closed the door behind them, shutting out the light from the hallway. They stood in darkness for several seconds while he groped for the light switch just inside the door. When the light went on, Molly seemed surprised that he hadn't tried to kiss her in the dark.

"This is very nice," she said, looking around the room. "Very nice."

"Thank you," he said. They were both whispering. No one had seen them come into the building, and no one knew she was here in the room with him, but they whispered nonetheless, as though the entire building knew they were alone together, as though each and every one of the tenants was eavesdropping.

"It's not too small at all," Molly said.

"No, it's all right. Plenty of room for just one person."

"That's right," Molly said. She took off her coat and scarf and put them over the arm of the easy chair. "Well," she said, "this is really nice. Maybe I'll move. Do you think there are any vacancies?"

"Gee, I wouldn't know," Roger said. "But actually, this room'll be empty tomorrow, you know. I'll be going back to Carey tomorrow."

"That's right," she said, "I almost forgot."

"Yeah," Roger said, and nodded.

She sat on the edge of the bed. "It's too bad you're going back so soon," she said.

"Well, there's really no reason for me to stay any longer, you know. My mother's expecting me, so really I have to—"

"Oh, sure," Molly said. "This is very comfortable. The bed."

"Yeah, it's not a bad bed," Roger said.

"It seems very comfortable. I hate lumpy mattresses, don't you?"

"Yes."

"Or ones that are too soft."

"This one is pretty good, actually," Roger said. "You get a good night's sleep on it."

Molly leaned back suddenly, swinging her legs up on to the bed and stretching her arms over her head. "Mmmm," she said, "this sure feels good." She smiled at Roger. "I'd better be careful or I'll fall asleep."

"Well," Roger said, and smiled.

"Do you know what gets me about looking for a job?" she asked.

"No what?"

"My feet. They're killing me. Would you mind if I took off my shoes?"

"No, not at all."

"I'll be leaving in a minute," she said, sitting up, and crossing her legs, and taking off first one high-heeled pump and then the other. "But while I'm here I might as well take advantage of the opportunity, huh?"

"Sure," Roger said.

"Ahhhhh," she said, and wiggled her toes. "Ahhhh, that feels good." She put her arms behind her, the elbows locked, and stared up at him. "Aren't you going to take off your coat?" she asked.

"What? Oh. Oh, I thought—"

"I've got a few minutes," she said. "We don't have to rush right out again. I mean, not unless you want to."

"No, no," Roger said.

"Besides, it feels so good with these shoes off," she said, and smiled.

"Just make yourself comfortable," he said. He took off his coat and went to the closet with it. "I'm sorry I can't offer you a drink or anything, but I haven't got any in the room."

"Oh, that's all right," she said. "I don't drink much anyway."

He hung his coat on a hanger, and then took Molly's from the chair and put it over his on the same hanger. He looped her scarf over the hanger hook, and put everything back in the closet. "If the liquor stores were open," he said, "I'd go down for some. But I think—"

"No, I don't mind. I hope I didn't give you the impression that I drink a lot."

"No, I didn't get that impression."

"Because I usually don't, except socially. It's been so depressing, though, marching around this city and not being able to find anything. It can get really depressing, I mean it."

"I can imagine," Roger said.

"Boy, it's good to get out of those shoes," she said, and she leaned back, propping herself on one elbow so she could watch him. She smiled. "Is that the only light in here?" she asked.

"What?"

"The light. It's kind of harsh."

"There's a lamp on the dresser," Roger said. "Would you like it better if I—"

"Please. It's just that lying back like this, I'm looking right up into the light there."

"I'll just put this one on," Roger said, and went to the dresser. He turned on the small lamp, and then flicked out the overhead light. "How's that?"

"Better," she said. "Much better."

She closed her eyes. The room was silent.

"Mmm," she said. She stretched and then leaned back and said, "I really better be careful or I *will* fall asleep."

"It's early yet," Roger said.

"The night is young, huh?" she said, and giggled. "Be funny if your landlady walked in here tomorrow morning and found a strange girl in your bed, wouldn't it?"

"Well, she never walks in," Roger said. "Nobody ever bothers you here."

"You mean you've had strange girls in here before?"

"No, I didn't mean *that*," Roger said.

The girl giggled. "I know. I'm teasing." She opened her eyes and looked at him solemnly. "I'm a big tease."

Roger said nothing.

"Though not that way," Molly said. She paused. "Do you know what I mean?"

"I'm not sure."

She smiled briefly, and then sat up suddenly, swung her legs over the side of the bed and said, "I'm getting your bedspread all wrinkled. Your landlady won't like that a bit. I mean, she may not object to girls in your room, but I'll bet she doesn't like a wrinkled bedspread or lipstick all over the pillow."

"Well, she's never found any lipstick on the pillow," Roger said, and smiled.

"No, and we're not going to *give* her any to find, either." She padded to the dresser in her stockinged feet, opened her bag, took out a Kleenex, and leaned close to the mirror. She wiped off her lipstick quickly, and then put the tissue back into her bag. "There," she said, and smiled at him. He was beginning to dislike the way she was making herself so comfortable, the way she was moving around the room so easily and naturally, as if she owned the place. He watched her as she went to the bed and pulled back the bedspread and fluffed up the pillows. "There," she said again, and sat on the edge of the bed.

She smiled at him.

"Well," she said, "here we are."

The room was silent again. She stared at him levelly.

"Do you want to make love to me?" she asked.

"That's not why I brought you up here," he said quickly.

The smile was still on her face, but it seemed to have weakened somewhat, as though his words had embarrassed her, or injured her. He didn't want to make her feel bad, and he certainly didn't want to hurt her. But at the same time, he didn't particularly feel like getting involved with her, not in that way, not with a girl as plain as she was.

"I mean, I didn't bring you up here to take advantage of you," he said gallantly. "I only wanted to show you the room because you said maybe you—"

"I know."

"—might want to move if it was a good-sized room."

"It's a good-sized room," she said.

"But, believe me, I wasn't planning—"

"And it's a very comfortable bed," she said.

"—on taking advantage of you, if that's what you thought."

"That's not what I thought."

"Good because—"

"I didn't think you'd take advantage of me."

"Good because—"

"It wouldn't be taking advantage of me," Molly said flatly.

He looked at her silently.

"I have a lot to give," she said.

He did not answer her.

She stood up suddenly and pulled the flaps of her blouse out of the black skirt. Slowly, she began unbuttoning the blouse. There was something ludicrous about her performance. She stood alongside the bed with her head erect, the flaming red hair burnished in the glow of the single lamp on the dresser, her hands slowly unbuttoning the blouse, staring at him, her eyes serious and solemn in the plain face, the fake eyelashes, the penciled eyebrows, the pointed fake breasts in the padded bra slowly revealed as her hands worked the buttons at the front of the blouse. She threw the blouse and the bra onto the bed behind her and then unzipped the skirt and stepped out of it. He felt nothing. He looked at her as she took off the rest of her clothing and moved toward him, an oddly shaped woman with tiny breasts, large bursting nipples, wide in the hips, far too wide in the behind, thick in the thigh and ankle, there was nothing exciting about her, nothing attractive about her, he felt no desire at all for her. She moved into his arms. She was very warm.

They whispered in the night.

"I sometimes feel all alone in the world," she said.

"I do, too."

"I don't mean alone just because I have no parents, or because Doris went off to Hawaii, not that way, not that kind of alone. I mean *really* alone."

"Yes."

"Alone inside," she said.

"Yes."

"Even when I'm surrounded by people. Even when there are people everywhere around me, like in that bar tonight, before I met you."

"I almost didn't come over to you."

"Because I'm not pretty," she said.

"You're beautiful," he said.

"No, please . . ."

"Yes."

"Please don't lie to me."

"You're the most beautiful girl I've ever known in my life."

"Ahhh," she said.

"Yes."

"Ahhh."

"Molly, you're beautiful," he whispered.

"I'm a good lay, is what you mean?"

"Yes, you're a good lay, but—"

"Mmmm, and that's it."

"No."

"Yes, that's all of it. Roger, please, I *know*."

"How do you know?"

She shrugged. "You're a man. I know what men want."

"That's not all I want," he said.

She moved closer to him. She buried her face in his shoulder. Her lips vibrated against his skin as she spoke. "You're the only man who ever told me I was beautiful," she whispered. She paused for a long time. "Roger?"

"Yes?"

"Tell me."

"What?"

"Tell me again."

"What?"

"Don't make me beg."

"You're beautiful," he said.

"You embarrass me," she whispered.

"I want to hold you," he said.

"Ahhh."

"I want to kiss you."

She moved into his arms. "What's this?" she whispered.

"Nothing."

"Nothing?" she whispered. "Oh, it's something. Oh, I can *tell* it's something. Oh, I'm *sure* it's something. Oh yes. Yes, yes, that's it, yes."

"Molly, Molly . . ."

"Ooooh, kiss you," she whispered. "Ooooh, hold you, kiss you, kiss you."

"Beautiful," he whispered, "beautiful."

Her scarf was in the bottom drawer of the dresser. He walked to the dresser now and opened the drawer and took out the scarf and held it in his hands. It was a pale-blue scarf, light, almost transparent, made of nylon, he supposed, he didn't really know. It was the only article of her clothing left behind in the apartment. He had discovered it afterward near the closet door, he supposed it had dropped from the hanger when he'd gone to get her coat.

He looked at the scarf and wondered what he should do with it. Suppose those two detectives came back to ask more questions, suppose they search the room? Well, no, they needed a warrant to do that, didn't they? Or did they? Suppose they came back while he was out with Amelia? He'd have to get rid of the scarf, that was for sure. Or else, he could simply take it with him when he went to the police station to tell them about it, yes, that would make things a lot simpler, sure. He would go there with the scarf and that would make it easier to talk about Molly. He would ask for the detective with the deaf-mute wife. He hadn't really liked any of the others, not Parker in the luncheonette, and not those two who had just been here, either, although they weren't too bad – still, he preferred the one with the beautiful wife.

Amelia, he thought.

I'd better get rid of this scarf, first, he thought, and wondered how he should do it.

I suppose I can cut it into little pieces and flush it down the toilet. That would probably be best. Only trouble is I haven't got a scissors, nor even a knife. I can tear it in my hands, I suppose.

He looked at the scarf again.

He grasped it firmly in both hands and tried to rip it, but it wouldn't start because there was a tight, strong welting all around the edge of it. He put the end of the scarf into his mouth and tore the welting with his teeth, and then ripped it in half along a jagged line, and then decided throwing it down the toilet wouldn't be any good. Suppose the damn toilet got stuffed, that would be just great.

He went to the dresser. A book of matches was lying in the ash tray near the lamp. He picked up the matches and went to the bathroom with the scarf. He struck a match, and then held the scarf hanging from one hand over the toilet bowl, almost touching the water. He brought the other hand, with the lighted match, toward the dangling end of the scarf and was about to set fire to it when he heard someone calling him.

He recognized Mrs. Dougherty's voice, and wondered how in hell she had known he was about to set fire to a scarf in her bathroom. He shook out the match and dropped it into the bowl, and went back to his room. There he wadded the scarf into a ball and put it into the bottom dresser drawer again.

Mrs. Dougherty was still yelling his name in the hallway. "Mr. Broome, Mr. Broome, Mr. Broome!"

He went to the door and opened it.

"Yes," he said, "what is it?"

"Mr. Broome, there's a phone call for you."

"What?" he said.

"The telephone," she said.

"Who is it?" he asked.

"I don't know. It's a woman."

My mother, he thought, and wondered how she had got the number.

"I'll be right down," he said. He closed the door, went back into the room, opened the bottom dresser drawer, and shoved the blue scarf all the way to the back of it. Then he closed the drawer and went out into the hall. The pay phone was on the wall of the first-floor landing. Mrs. Dougherty was standing near the phone, waiting for him.

"Did the detectives talk to you?" she asked.

"Yes," he said.

"They were nice boys, weren't they?"

"Yes, they seemed very nice. Are they still in the building?"

"They're talking to Mrs. Ingersol on the fifth floor."

"Then they're almost finished, I guess," Roger said. He took the receiver from her hand. "Thank you," he said.

"Do you think they'll get my refrigerator back?" Mrs. Dougherty asked.

"I hope so," Roger said, and he smiled and put the receiver to his ear. "Hello?"

Mrs. Dougherty smiled and nodded and started down the steps to her apartment on the ground floor just as the voice at his ear said, "Roger, is it you? This is Amelia."

"Amelia? How – *Amelia*, did you say?"

"I was hoping you hadn't left yet."

"No, I'm still here. What time is it?"

"It's three-twenty. I was afraid you might have left."

"Why? What's the matter?"

"I'm going to be a little late."

"Why?"

"Something unexpected."

"Like what?"

"I'll tell you when I see you."

"How late will you be?"

"Four-thirty?" she said. "Is that *too* late?"

"No, that's fine."

"Same place?"

"Yes, outside the drugstore."

"Aren't you curious?"

"About what?"

"About how I got your phone number?"

"Yeah, how about that?" he said.

"Some memory, huh?"

"What do you mean? I never gave you the number here. I don't even know the number here myself."

"Aha," she said.

"How'd you get it?"

"Agnes Dougherty," she said.

"What?"

"The name on one of your valentines. The cards. Remember?"

"Oh, yeah, that's right," he said, smiling.

"Your landlady."

"That's right."

"Or so you said."

"She is. I'll introduce you to her, if you like."

"When?"

"Later."

"Sure," Amelia said. "You can't kid me. She's some big old blond broad you're living with, you can't kid me."

"No," he said, grinning, "she's my landlady."

"Hey, you know something?"

"What?"

"I like you."

"I like you, too, Amelia."

"Good."

"Four-thirty, okay?"

"Yes." She paused. "Roger?"

"Yes?"

"I *more* than just like you."

"Okay."

"Okay, look at the brushoff," she said, and laughed.

"What brushoff?"

"You're supposed to say you *more* than just like me, too."

"I do."

"Ah, such enthusiasm," Amelia said. "Okay, I'll see you later. You think you can keep out of trouble between now and four-thirty?"

"I'll try," Roger said.

"Yeah, try," she answered. "Try real hard."

"I will."

"You're very cute," she said, and hung up.

He stood grinning at the receiver for a moment, and then replaced it on the cradle.

He went up to the apartment then and burned Molly's scarf and flushed the ashes down the toilet, and then opened the bathroom window to let out the smoke.

11

The snow had stopped.

There was a silence to the city.

There was a clean silence that reached somewhere deep inside him the moment he stepped outside and began walking toward the garage. His footfalls were hushed, his breath plumed out ahead of him in visible silence, there was the normal hush of late afternoon, the whispering minutes before twilight, intensified now by the cushion of snow, deepened, the gentle rhythmic sound of skid chains, muffled. I'll have to put chains on the truck, he thought.

The thought came into his mind with a suddenness that was totally surprising because it carried with it the idea of going home; if he was planning to put chains on the truck, then he was planning to *use* the truck, to go someplace with it, and the only place he would take the truck would be home to Carey. He knew that was what he ought to do, put chains on the truck, and then call his mother and tell her he was leaving the city, probably be home this evening sometime, that was the thing to do. But there were also a few other things he knew he should do, or at least *felt* he ought to do, and suddenly everything seemed mixed up, suddenly the silence of the city was irritating to him rather than soothing. He knew he should call his mother and then head for home, and he also knew he should go to the police station and talk to that detective with the deaf-and-dumb wife, but he also knew he should meet Amelia at four-thirty because Amelia was the most beautiful woman he had ever known in his life and he had the feeling he should not allow her to get away from him, colored or otherwise. It still bothered him that she was colored, but not as much as it had bothered him earlier. He thought suddenly of Molly and how she had become beautiful all at once at two o'clock last night, but that was something different, that wasn't the way he felt about Amelia, that was something entirely different. Amelia really *was* beautiful, everything *about* her was beautiful – the way she looked, and the soft way she had of speaking, and that fine bright quickness about her, and the way she kissed, she really was a beautiful girl. His mother certainly wouldn't be able to kid about her the way she had kidded about all the ugly ducklings he took out in Carey, not by a long shot. It troubled him that he would be seeing Amelia when he knew he should be going home to his mother. After all, somebody had to take care of her now that his father was dead. But at the same time he really *did* want to see Amelia, to *know* Amelia, and this frightened him because at some point last night when he was in bed with Molly he had begun to think that he would really like to know her, too, and not just as somebody to take to bed, some ugly girl to take to bed, but as a beautiful person secret and private inside this very plain outside shell. That was when he supposed he began to get angry with her, that was when he supposed the argument started.

He did not want an argument to start with Amelia, and yet he had the feeling that if he met her later on he would argue with her, too, and all because he knew he should be home in Carey taking care of his mother and not getting involved with pretty girls in the city, especially pretty girls who were colored. He didn't see how he could get involved with a colored girl. Hell, he wouldn't even have asked her to take the afternoon off if he'd thought there was the slightest possibility of getting involved with someone who was colored. But then he hadn't thought he'd get involved with anyone as ugly as Molly, either, until he found himself really wondering about her and looking at her as if she was beautiful, and really believing she was beautiful, that was what had caused all the trouble.

So the thing he should do, he supposed, was to go to the police and tell them about Molly, and then go home to Carey. No, that wouldn't exactly work, either. Going to the police would keep him away from Amelia, would keep him from getting involved with her, or of getting angry with her the way he'd got angry with Molly, but it would also keep him away from his mother in Carey, well, maybe that wouldn't be so bad. He was suddenly very confused.

Look, he told himself, I'd better

Look, I think the police

Well, look, let me put the chains on the truck for now. Let me do that, and I'll work out the rest.

I mean, what the hell, she's sitting all the way up there, *somebody's* got to take care of her.

Buddy's just a kid.

Somebody's got to take care of her.

The garage attendant was a short fellow with curly black hair and very white teeth. He was wearing an old World War II flight jacket, the same jacket he'd been wearing the other day when Roger pulled in with the truck loaded.

"Hey," he said, "how you doing?"

"Fine," Roger said. "I just thought I'd stop by to put my chains on. I wasn't expecting this kind of snow."

"Something, huh?" the attendant said. "You could freeze your ass off in this city."

"It gets a lot colder up where I live," Roger said.

"Yeah, where you live?" the attendant asked, grinning. "Siberia? Or Lower Slobovia, which?"

Roger didn't know where Lower Slobovia was, so he just said, "Well, it gets pretty cold up there, believe me."

"I see you got rid of all your stuff," the attendant said.

"Yes. I sold it all yesterday."

"That's good, huh?"

"Yes, that's fine," Roger said.

"Late last night?" the attendant said.

"What?"

"That when you sold it?"

"No. No," Roger said. He stared at the attendant, puzzled. "I don't think I get you."

"The benches and stuff, the bowls. You know?"

"Yes?"

"Did you sell them late last night?"

"No. I sold the last of them yesterday afternoon sometime. Downtown."

"Oh."

"Why?"

"Oh, nothing," the attendant said. "Only I must've been gone when you came back, and the night man said you took the truck out again later."

"He did?"

"Yeah. He only told me about it because he wasn't sure he should have let it go out, you know, so he was just checking. To make sure he didn't pull a boner. You know?"

"Mmm," Roger said.

"That was pretty late."

"Yes."

"Three o'clock in the morning." The attendant grinned. His teeth were very white. "Or *early*, depending how you look at it, huh? Three o'clock could be very early."

"It *was* early," Roger said. "I had to carry some stuff."

"More of that wood stuff, huh?"

"No," Roger said quickly. "I . . ." He paused. "A man offered me a job. Yesterday afternoon, while I was downtown."

"Oh? Yeah?"

"Hauling some vegetables for him. From the market."

"Hey, that's a lucky break, huh?" the attendant said.

"Yes, I had to take them over the bridge to the other side of the river. Over there. I had to pick them up at the market."

"Downtown, huh?"

"Yes."

"Where? Down near Cummings?"

"What?"

"Cummings Street? The market down there?"

"Yes, the market."

"Sure, they open very early," the attendant said.

"Yes, I had to be there at three-thirty to make the pickup. And then I had to drive all way to the bridge and across the river."

"All the way to Lower Slobovia, huh?" the attendant said, and laughed. "Well, you're a hard worker, that's good. I admire guys who are willing to work to earn a buck. Christ knows I work hard enough. Your truck's over there near that '62 Caddy. You want a hand with the chains?"

"No, I think I can manage. Thanks."

"Don't mention it. You want the keys?"

"I don't know. How much space have I got?"

"I think you can get them on without moving it. But if you need the keys, they're right here on the board."

"Okay," Roger said, and walked to where the truck was parked at the far end of the garage. He glanced at the Cadillac alongside it, and then lowered the tailgate and climbed up into the back. His chains were in the right-hand forward corner of the truck, up near the cab, wrapped in burlap. He always dried them carefully each time he took them off, and then wrapped them in burlap so they wouldn't rust. He picked up the chains and was heading for the rear of the truck again when he saw the stain.

The stain was no larger than a half-dollar, circular, with a sawtooth edge and tiny spatters radiating from the rim.

That must've been from her nose, he thought.

He climbed down from the truck and dropped the chains near the left rear wheel, and then looked around the garage and saw a hose attached to a faucet, and alongside that a can. He glanced toward the front of the garage to check if the attendant was anywhere in sight. He walked to the hose and picked up the can and filled it about a quarter full, and then went back to the truck again. He put the can down near the tailgate. From under the front seat he took an old soiled rag, and he carried that with him to the back of the truck again, where he dipped it into the can of water.

He was very lucky. The blood had dripped onto one of the metal strips running the length of the truck, and had not fallen on the wooden floor of the body. It might have been difficult to remove a bloodstain from a wooden floor. Instead, he wiped the blood off the metal in as long as it took him to pass the wet cloth over it.

He rinsed the cloth out several times until it was clean. The water in the can showed hardly any discoloration, hardly any trace of red or even pink. He poured the water down the open drain near the hose attachment, and rinsed the can out several times.

He went back to the truck and put on the chains.

She was waiting for him outside the drugstore.

She spotted him as he turned the corner, and waved immediately and came running up to him.

"Hi," she said, and looped her arm through his. "You're late."

"I haven't got a watch," he said.

"Well, you're not *too* late, it's only about twenty to. Where were you?"

"Putting chains on my truck."

"Fine thing. Guy'd rather put chains on his truck than be with me."

"No, I'd rather be with you, Amelia."

"There are times, you know," she said, smiling, "when I think you have absolutely no sense of humor."

"None at all," he said, and returned her smile.

"So look at me," she said.

He looked at her.

"Well?"

"You changed your coat."

"This is my best coat. I only wear it on very special occasions. The collar is genuine fitch."

"What's fitch?"

"An animal."

"I know that, but—"

"You've never heard of rat fitch?"

"No."

"It's a close relative to rat fink. There are millions of rat finks in this city, but only very few rat fitches. One of them voluntarily donated his life to make a collar for my coat. Stunning, isn't it?"

"Stunning."

"Also, look." She unbuttoned the coat and held it open, her arms widespread. She was wearing a black skirt and a V-necked black sweater cut very low over her breasts. A string of tiny pearls circled her throat, startling white against her dark skin. "Very sexy number, huh?" she said.

"Very sexy."

"Also," she said, and winked, "black bra underneath. Men like black bras, huh?"

"Yes."

"Now, if you don't mind, I'll close the coat before I freeze everything I own, you don't mind, huh?" She closed the coat and buttoned it. "Brrrr, my hands are freezing." She put her left hand into the pocket of her coat, and then entwined the fingers of her right hand in his, and put both their hands into the pocket of his coat. "There," she said, "nice and cozy and warm, I can't stop talking, what the hell is it about you?"

"I'm a good listener," he said, "that's what it is."

"Yeah, how come?"

"In my house, I listen all the time."

"To who?"

"My mother."

"Mmm, mothers, don't talk about mothers. You should hear the lecture I got this afternoon."

"About what?"

"About *you*, what do you think?"

"Why?"

"Man, you de white man. You Mr. Charlie." Amelia giggled.

"Is that what Mr. Charlie is?"

"Well, sure. You Mr. Charlie, and you de ofay, and you sometimes just De Man, although De Man is also sometimes a plain old pusher, but he usually a *white* man, too, so I guess you synonymous, is that de word, man?"

"I don't know."

"It went on for hours, I thought she'd never stop."

"Is that why you couldn't make it at three-thirty?"

"That's why. She had my brother come over to talk to me. He's married and has two kids, and he drives a cab. So she called his garage and asked them to tell him to call his mother as soon as he checked in. He doesn't check in 'til about four, so I knew I'd be stuck there 'til at least a quarter after, his garage is on Twentieth, near the river. Anyway, he got to the house at twenty-five after, and I talked to him for about three seconds flat and then left."

"What'd he say?"

"He said, 'Amelia, you are out of your head.'"

"What did you say?"

"I said, 'Louis, go to hell.'"

"And then what?"

"He said if he caught us together he would cut off your balls."

"Will he really?"

"Louis is a fat happy cab driver who wouldn't know where to *find* your balls because he hasn't had any of his own since the day he married Mercedes in 1953, do you mind my talking this way?"

"What way?"

"Well, I swear a lot, I guess. Although, actually, I'm only repeating what my brother said. Anyway, I told him to go to hell again, and I walked out."

"I don't mind," Roger said.

"What do you mean?"

"Your swearing a lot." He paused. "We never swear in our house. My mother's pretty strict about that."

"Well, the hell with mothers, huh?" she said.

He felt a momentary spark of anger, and then he simply nodded. "What would you like to do?" he asked.

"Walk a little. I love snow. It makes me stand out."

"You stand out anyway," he said.

"Do I?"

"Yes."

"You say very sweet things, sweet-talker. Mother warned me. Oops, excuse me, we're not supposed to talk about mothers."

"Where would you like to walk?"

"Any place, who cares?"

He didn't like the way Amelia said that, but he told himself not to get angry. She was, after all, allowing him to assume the responsibility. She was saying she would follow him wherever he wanted to go. She was allowing him to be the man. It's *you* who's the man in the family now, Roger. He did not want to get angry with her the way he had got angry with Molly last night. Last night, he had begun to get angry with Molly when she started telling him about that man in Sacramento. He told himself later that she should not have begun talking about another man when she was in bed with him. That was what had got him so angry. But he had the feeling, even while he was trying to convince himself, that the *real* reason for his sudden anger had nothing at all to do with the man in Sacramento. He couldn't quite understand it, but he knew somehow he had got angry with Molly only because he was beginning to like her so much. That was the part he couldn't understand.

"There's been only one other man in my life who mattered," Molly had said last night. "Before you. Only one other."

He said nothing. They were lying naked on the bed in his room, and he felt spent and exhausted and content, listening to the February wind howling outside, wind always sounded more fierce in the dead of night, especially in a strange city.

"I met him when I was twenty, just a year after my mother passed away, do you mind my talking about this?"

"No," he said, because he really didn't mind yet, he wasn't angry with her yet, he liked her very much. He kept thinking about how his mother would make fun of him for bringing home another ugly duckling and of how he would say, "Why Mom, she's beautiful, what's the matter with you?"

"It was the first job after secretarial school, I really didn't know how to handle either the job *or* him. I never went out much with boys, boys hardly ever asked me out. I think I'd been kissed maybe half a dozen times in my life, and once a boy touched my breast when we were decorating the high school gym for a senior dance. I didn't even go to the dance because no one asked me." She paused. "His name was Theodore Michelsen, he had a brother who was a priest in San Diego. He was married and had two children, a little boy and a little girl, their pictures were on his desk. His wife's picture was on his desk, too, in the same frame, one of those frames that open like a book. His wife was on the left-hand side and his two children on the right. Do you mind my talking about this?"

"No," he said. He didn't mind. He was lying with his arm around her, and her lips close to his ear, staring up at the ceiling and thinking how soft her voice was and how warm and smooth she felt in his arms.

"I don't know how it started," Molly said. "I guess one day he just kissed me, and I guess it was the first time I'd ever really been kissed by anyone, I mean really kissed by a man. And then, I don't know, we just began, not that same day, but a few days later, I guess it was a Friday, I guess it was after everyone had gone home. We made love in his office, look, I know you don't want to hear this."

"No, that's all right," he said.

"We did it every day," she said. "I loved it," she said.

That was when he got angry.

He could hear the snow squeaking under his shoes. Amelia held his arm tightly and said, "We're heading for the river, did you know that?"

"No, I didn't."

"What were you thinking?"

"Thinking?" He shook his head. "Nothing."

"Oh, *yes* you were. Just a few minutes ago. You were a million miles away."

"I was thinking I ought to be getting home."

"I must be a real fascinating girl. You're walking with me, and all you can think about is getting home."

"I didn't mean it that way. It's just my mother's all alone up there. Not really alone, I have a younger brother, but you know."

"Yes," Amelia said.

"It's just I'm the man in the family."

"Yes."

"That's all." He shrugged.

"Still, you *are* here," she said. "You *are* with me."

"Yes, I know. I'm sorry. I shouldn't have—"

"I mean, I *am* a fairly good-looking girl, you know, what with my rat-fitch collar and my sexy black sweater." She grinned. "I mean well, you know, a girl doesn't get all dressed up so some guy can think of running back home to Gulchwater Flats."

"Carey," he said, and smiled.

"Right?"

"Right."

"So what do you intend to do about it, look, there's ice on the river, you could probably walk clear across to the other shore."

"There wasn't any ice last night," he said.

"What?"

"Nothing."

"Were you here last night?"

"Well, I meant early this morning. About three o'clock."

"What were you doing here at three in the morning?"

"I wasn't *here*."

"But you said—"

"I had to make a delivery."

"A delivery?"

"Yes. Vegetables."

"Oh."

"So I had a chance to see the river, that's all I meant."

"And there was no ice."

"No. I guess it must have been a little above freezing."

"It felt a lot colder than that yesterday," she said.

"Yes, it did. But the river wasn't frozen."

"Okay," she said. "You want to walk across to the other side?"

"No."

"Vegetables, did you say?"

"Yes, I got the job from a man, to pick up these vegetables and deliver them. With my truck."

"Oh." She nodded, and then said, "How cold do you think it is now?"

"I don't know. In the twenties, I'd guess."

"Are you cold?"

"A little."

"My feet are cold," she said.

"You want to go someplace? For coffee or something?"

"I thought you had a room," she said.

"I do."

"Let's go there."

They walked in silence for several moments. The river was frozen from shore to shore. The bridge uptown spanned the ice, rose from the ice as if it were a silvery spidery extension of it.

"I don't want to hurt you," he said.

"Hurt me? How can you hurt me?"

"I don't know," he said, and shrugged.

"Honey," she said, "I've been had by experts."

"Amelia, there are . . ." He shook his head.

"Yes? What?"

"There are a lot of things . . ." He shook his head again.

"What is it, Roger?"

"I should do."

"What?"

"Things I should do."

"Yes, like what?"

"Well . . . I want to be with you."

"Yes, I want to be with you, too."

"I want to kiss you again, I've been wanting to ever since—"

"Yes, yes—"

"But I don't want to hurt you."

"But, baby, how can you possibly—"

"I just want you to know that."

She stared at him silently. At last she said, "You're a funny person." She reached up and kissed him swiftly and then moved back from him and looked into his face and said, "Come," and took his hand.

12

The party in Roger's room started at about five-thirty when Fook Shanahan came in with a man who lived on the second floor and whom Roger didn't know at all. He and Amelia had just come into the room, had in fact barely taken off their coats when Fook knocked on the door and – without waiting for anyone to answer – opened the door and came in, followed by a very tall thin man with thick-rimmed eyeglasses and a thatch of brown hair turning white. His eyebrows were already completely white, thick and shaggy; they looked fake to Roger, as if they had been pasted on as a disguise. Fook had a bottle of bourbon in one hand, and two glasses in the other. He went immediately to the dresser where he put down the bottle and the glasses and then he turned to Roger and said, "Aren't you going to introduce us to the young lady?"

"Oh, sure," Roger said. "This is Amelia Perez. Amelia, I'd like you to meet Fook Shanahan, and I'm afraid I don't know the other gentleman's name."

"The other gentleman's name is Dominick Tartaglia," Fook said, "and he's no gentleman, believe me." Tartaglia laughed. Fook laughed with him and then said, "I gather you two have just come in from the frozen tundra out there, and would appreciate a drink."

"Well . . ." Roger said hesitantly, and then glanced at Amelia.

"Sure," Amelia said. "I'd love a drink."

"The problem is one of numerical disproportion," Fook said. "We seem to have four people and only three glasses."

"Roger and I can share a glass," Amelia said, and smiled gently at him.

"Then there's no problem," Fook said. He went to the dresser and opened the bottle. Amelia sat on the edge of the bed, crossing her legs and leaning forward, resting her elbow on her knee, one hand toying with the pearls at her throat. Tartaglia stood alongside the dresser, smiling as Fook poured the drinks. Roger glanced at Amelia to see if she minded them being here, but she seemed to be pretty happy. We'll make love as soon as they leave, he thought.

And suddenly he was frightened.

"We were waiting for you to come home, Roger," Fook said, "because we wanted to know how you made out with the bulls."

"Oh, we had a nice talk," Roger said.

"Were the police here?" Amelia asked, and she suddenly sat up straight and looked at Roger.

"Yeah," Tartaglia said. "Our landlady had a refrigerator stolen from her."

"A refrigerator?" Amelia said. "Thank you," she said to Fook as he handed her the drink.

"I apologize for the lack of ice," Fook said. "Would you like a little water in that?"

"Spoils the taste," Amelia said, and grinned.

"Ah, an Irish colored girl," Shanahan said. "The best kind." He lifted his glass. "Cheers, Miss."

Amelia sipped at her drink and then raised her eyebrows and rolled her eyes. "Whoosh!" she said, and handed the glass to Roger. Roger sniffed it, and then took a short swallow.

"So what happened?" Fook asked.

"Nothing," Roger said. "They came in and they were very polite, and they asked me where I'd been last night, and I told them. Then, let me see, I guess we talked about how much I thought the refrigerator was worth, and then they said I could go home or stay here, whichever I wanted, they had no more questions for me."

"That means they think he's clean," Tartaglia said to Fook.

"Of *course*," Fook said. "We're *all* clean. Who the hell would want to steal that old bitch's box, excuse me, Miss."

"That's all right," Amelia said, and she took another sip of the drink.

"Did you tell him about the shelves?" Tartaglia said.

"No," Fook said.

"What about the shelves?"

"They found them."

"What shelves?" Amelia asked.

"From the refrigerator. They found them near the furnace downstairs," Tartaglia said.

"Which means," Fook said, "that whoever went to the trouble of stealing that broken-down piece of machinery *also* went to the trouble of removing the shelves from it first. Now does that make any sense to you?"

"None at all," Amelia said, and finished her drink.

"Are you ready for another one, young lady?" Tartaglia asked.

"Just to take off the chill," Amelia said, and she winked.

"She's Irish, I tell you," Fook said.

Tartaglia took her glass and poured it half full. He poured more bourbon into his own glass, and then handed Amelia hers and walked to Fook with the bottle, filling his glass as Fook talked.

"What good is a refrigerator without shelves?" Fook asked. "You're not drinking, Roger. You're supposed to be sharing the young lady's drink."

"Amelia," she said.

"Yes, Amelia, of course. You're a beautiful girl, Amelia," Fook said. "May I congratulate you upon your taste, Roger?"

"Yes, you may," Roger said, and smiled.

"Congratulations," Fook said. "Isn't there another glass in this place?"

"I'm afraid not."

"I insist that you share the lady's—"

"Amelia," she said.

"Yes, I insist that you share *Amelia's* drink. *Amelia*, let the man have a sip."

"Well, I don't want to drink too much," Roger said.

"He gets violent when he's drunk," Fook said, and winked at Amelia.

"No, I don't think so," she said. "I don't think he's that kind."

"No, he's a very sweet man," Fook said, taking the glass from her gently, and handing it to Roger. "Drink," he said. "And tell me what you think about those shelves."

Roger sipped at the bourbon and then handed the glass back to Amelia. "Gee, I don't know what to make of it," he said.

"Why would anyone steal a refrigerator and leave the shelves behind?" Fook asked.

"Maybe it was too heavy to carry with the shelves in it," Tartaglia said, and burst out laughing.

"Let me get this straight," Amelia said, drinking. "A refrigerator was stolen from your landlady's apartment last night, but the shelves—"

"From the basement," Tartaglia corrected. "It was stolen from the basement."

"Oh. I see. Oh. But in any case, whoever took it first removed the shelves from inside, is this right?"

"That's right."

"Fingerprints." Amelia said.

"Of course!" Fook said.

"They'll find fingerprints on the shelves," Tartaglia said. "That's right. You're right, miss, have another drink."

"I'll get plotzed," Amelia said. "You'll get me plotzed here, I won't know what the hell I'm doing." She held out her glass.

They won't find fingerprints on the shelves, Roger thought. I was wearing gloves. They won't find fingerprints anywhere in that basement.

"But why did he take out the shelves?" Fook insisted. "That's the problem. Fingerprints aside, why did he bother to remove the shelves?"

They were all silent, thinking.

"I don't know," Amelia said at last, and took another swallow of bourbon.

"I don't know, either," Tartaglia said.

"Nor I," Fook said.

"Roger?" Amelia said. She grinned somewhat foolishly, and cocked her head to one side, as though she were having trouble keeping him in focus. "You seem to have an idea."

"No," he said.

"You seemed very thoughtful there," she said.

"No."

"Didn't he seem very thoughtful there?" she asked.

"He certainly did," Tartaglia said.

"Well, I don't have any ideas," Roger said, and smiled.

"I have the feeling he would like us to get out of here," Fook said.

"No, no . . ."

"I have that feeling, too," Tartaglia said.

"I think we've overstayed our welcome," Fook said. "I'm sure Roger and Amelia have a great many things to talk about, and couldn't care less about Mrs. Dougherty's goddamn icebox."

"Refrigerator," Tartaglia said.

"Yes, pardon me," Fook said, "and pardon me for saying goddamn, Miss."

"Amelia."

"Yes, Amelia."

"You don't have to rush off," Roger said. "Have another drink."

"No, no, we simply wanted to know how you'd made out with those two bulls they sent over from the station house. What were their names, Dominick? Do you remember their names?"

"Mutt and Jeff," Tartaglia said, and laughed. "You think they're ever going to find that refrigerator?"

"Never," Fook said.

"You know what?"

"What?"

"I'll bet somebody's got that refrigerator in his kitchen right this minute. I'll bet it's full of beer and eggs and milk and soda and cheese and apples and oranges and bananas and grapes and jelly and—"

"Oh, you should never put ba-nan-nuhs," Amelia sang, "In the re-fridge-a-ray-ter!"

"Cha-cha-cha," Fook said, and laughed.

"And this guy probably lives right across the hall from a cop," Tartaglia continued, "and tonight this cop'll go in there for a glass of beer or something, and the guy'll go to his refrigerator he swiped and the cop'll sit there and not even know it's a hot refrigerator," he said, and burst out laughing.

"How can a refrigerator be hot?" Amelia asked, and began laughing.

"We've got to go," Fook said. He went to the dresser and picked up his bottle. "We're glad the police gave you a clean bill of health, Roger. The least you could do, however, is ask whether Dominick here and myself also passed muster."

"Oh, gee, I'm sorry," Roger said. "I didn't mean to—"

"You will be delighted to learn that we are neither of us suspects. In the considered opinion of the police, this was an outside job. As a matter of fact, they think the basement door was jimmied. The short one said so."

"Good night, Amelia," Tartaglia said from the door.

"Good night," she said.

"It was a pleasure meeting you," he said.

"Thank you. You, too."

"It was a pleasure," Tartaglia said again.

"Miss," Fook said, and he stopped in front of her and made a small bow. "You are with one of the sweetest people who ever walked the face of this earth, Roger Broome, a fine man even on short acquaintance."

"I know," Amelia said.

"Good. You are a fine woman."

"Thank you."

"Good," he said. He went to the door. "Be sweet to each other," he said. "You are very sweet people. Be sweet."

He made a short bow and then went out. Tartaglia went out behind him, closing the door.

"I think you had better lock it," Amelia said thickly.

"Why?"

"Mmm," she said, and grinned wickedly. "We have things to do, Roger. We have *nice* things to do." She rose unsteadily and walked to the closet door, opening it, and then pulling back in surprise and turning to him and covering her giggle with a cupped hand. "I thought it was the john," she said. "Where's the john?"

"Down the hall."

"Would you mind if I went to wash my face?" she asked.

"No, not at all," he said.

"I'll be right back," she said. She went to the door, opened it, turned, and then said – with great dignity – "I *really* have to pee," and went out.

Roger sat on the edge of the bed.

His hands were sweating.

He had hit Molly very suddenly.

He had not known he was going to hit her until his hand came out, not in an open-palmed slap, but the fist bunched instead into a tight hard ball. He had struck out and hit her in the eye, and then had pulled back his fist and hit her again, making her nose bleed. He saw her opening her mouth to scream, everything looked very peculiar all at once, the blood starting from her nose, he instinctively knew he could not allow any blood to stain the sheets, her mouth beginning to open in what he knew would be a piercing scream, he reached out quickly and grabbed her throat in both huge hands, squeezing. The scream died somewhere back in her throat, leaving only a small clicking gasp as his fingers closed on her neck. He lifted her off the bed at the same moment, bending her back so that the blood ran from her nose to the side of her face and over her jawbone and down her throat, over his hands – he almost released her when the blood touched his hands – and then down over her collarbone and her small naked breasts, but not touching the bed or the floor, he did not want bloodstains on anything. He wondered for a split instant – as her eyes bulged in her head, and she struck out at him with weakening hands, the hands fluttering aimlessly like broken butterflies – he wondered why he was doing this, he loved her, she was beautiful, why was he doing this, he hated her. Everything was bottled inside her head, everything was bulging into her head as he continued squeezing, blood was bursting from her nose, her eyes were getting wider and wider, her mouth opened, a curious retching sound came from her, he thought she would vomit on his hands, he almost backed away from her and then everything seemed to stop. He realized she was no longer struggling. She hung limp at the ends of his hands. He lowered her slowly to the floor, taking care that he did not tilt her head, not wanting to get any blood on anything. He left her naked, lying on her back, and went into the bathroom to wash his hands.

He sat with her for perhaps a half hour trying to figure out what he should do.

He thought maybe he should call his mother and tell her he had killed a girl. But then he had the funniest feeling his mother would just say Come home as quick as you can, son, leave her there and come home. He didn't think that was the right thing to do.

He kept looking at the girl lying naked on the floor. She looked even uglier in death, and he wondered how he could have ever thought she was beautiful, and then for a reason he could not understand, he reached down and with his forefinger he gently and tenderly traced the outline of her profile. Then he closed her staring eyes.

I'll take her to the police, he thought.

He went to the closet for her coat, thinking he couldn't carry her into a police station naked. He took the coat from the hanger and spread it on the floor beside her, and then lifted her and put her onto the coat as though it were a blanket, without making any attempt to put her arms into the sleeves. He went around the room then, picking up her clothing, the blouse, the skirt, the padded bra, the shoes she had taken off because her feet hurt from looking for a job, the panty-girdle, and folded these and put them all on her chest in a neat flat pile, leaving out only her nylons. He closed the coat over her chest. He did not button it. He took one of the nylons and slipped it under her back and her arms and then pulled it over her breasts and knotted it tightly. He wrapped the other nylon around her thighs, just above where the coat ended, and again knotted it tightly, and then looked down at the girl.

Her nose had stopped bleeding.

He couldn't just carry her in his arms, could he? In the street that way? He wondered what time it was. He supposed it was two o'clock or a little after, no, it wouldn't be right carrying her to the police station in his arms. No.

He didn't even know where the police station was.

He guessed he ought to go get the truck.

He could put her in the back of the truck.

He looked down at her once more where she lay trussed on the floor, one nylon tightly knotted over her breasts, holding the piled clothing in place under the coat, the other knotted around her thighs, her head sticking out of the top of the coat and her legs out of the bottom. He figured she'd be all right while he went to get the truck. He put on his coat and then went outside, testing the door behind him to make sure it was locked. He could hear Fook snoring in his room down the hall. He went down the steps quietly and cautiously and then came out into the street and began walking toward the garage. It was not as cold as it had been earlier. That surprised him. It was very windy, but the temperature wasn't all that bad. He walked with a quick spring in his step, the whole thing very clear in his mind. He would get the truck and back it down that alley alongside the building, into the back yard to the basement door. He knew there was a back door to the basement because he had seen the man from the electric company going down the alley to read the meter just yesterday. He had never been down in the basement, but he knew there was a door back there.

The night attendant at the garage wanted to know who he was, and he said he was Roger Broome and that he would like his truck, the '59 Chevy. The night man wasn't too keen on letting the truck go out at close to two-thirty in the morning, but Roger showed him the registration for the truck, and the night man sort of clucked his tongue and shook his head and said, Well, okay, I guess it's all right, I sure *hope* it's all right.

The streets were fairly deserted at that hour.

He backed the truck down the alley, cutting the engine at the top of the drive, and letting it roll back down, and then pulling the wheel sharply at the bottom of the drive so that the truck swung in close to the back of the building. He got out and saw the basement door at once. He tried the knob, but the door was locked. He walked back to the truck and took the lug wrench from under the front seat and then went to the door and kept prying at the area near the lock until the wood was splintered and jagged, and finally the lock snapped. He went into the basement and groped his way around until he found the steps leading to the ground floor of the building. He went up the steps without turning on any lights and felt for the lock on the door, and then opened the door and came into the hallway. He propped the door open by putting his truck keys on the floor in the narrow wedge where the door joined the jamb. Then he went upstairs to his room.

The girl was where he'd left her, lying on the floor.

He went to the bed and looked at it to see if there were any bloodstains on the sheets, and then he checked the floor for bloodstains, and then he looked around to make sure he'd got all of her clothes. He dragged her over to the door and opened it a crack and looked out into the hall. He didn't know why he was being so careful about bloodstains and clothes and looking out into the hallway, especially when his plan was to drive straight to the nearest police station and go in and tell them he'd killed this girl, that was going to be hard to do.

There was no one in the hallway, the building was asleep.

He picked her up, she was as light as a feather, and carried her into the hall, bracing her with one arm while he pulled the door shut with his free hand, and then holding her in both arms and going quickly down the steps to the basement door. He opened the door and then bent down for his truck keys, bracing the girl against his knee again. He went down the steps. The basement was illuminated with thin shafts of moonlight that glanced through the small side windows high up on the cinderblock wall. His eyes were becoming accustomed to the light. He could make out the furnace, and beyond that an old refrigerator, and beyond that a bicycle with one wheel. He carried Molly out of the basement and then put her into the back of the truck. A think trickle of blood had run from her nose to her upper lip. He was about to get into the truck cab and drive to the police station when he wondered what he would tell them. He stood in the silent back yard. Above him the clotheslines stretched from pole to pole, frantically and silently moving in the wind. Boy, it sure would be hard to go in there and tell them what had happened. He stood near the rear of the truck, staring at the girl wrapped in her own coat.

If he took her someplace

Well, he ought

Well

Well, what he ought to do was go to the police.

Still, if

No.

No, he had to get rid of her.

He kept looking at the girl.

Yes, he had to get rid of her.

He shrugged and went back into the basement. He went directly to the refrigerator he had seen and he opened the door and looked inside and knew immediately he would have to take the shelves out. The first two came out easily enough, but he had to struggle with the third one, and then the fourth came out just by lifting it. He put all four shelves alongside the furnace, and then he wrapped his arms around the refrigerator and tried to lift it. It was too heavy for him. He would never be able to carry it clear across the basement to the back door.

He wondered if he should forget about it.

Maybe he should take her to the police station after all.

He kept staring at the refrigerator.

Finally, he wrapped his arms around it again, but this time he lifted one end of the box and walked it forward and then lifted the opposite end, and kept doing that, shifting from one leg of the refrigerator to the other, walking it toward the door. At the door, he lifted it over the sill and then shoved it onto the concrete of the back yard and walked it to the tailgate of the truck. He wasn't at all tired. Walking the box out to the truck had been fairly simple, but he knew it would take all his strength to lift it up onto the tailgate and into the truck.

He looked at the girl.

He kept expecting her to move or something. Maybe open her eyes.

He bent at the knees and wrapped his arms around the refrigerator again and then braced himself and began lifting. The box slipped. He backed away from it in surprise. It made a dull heavy noise as it fell back to the concrete, upright. He gripped it again, and this time he mustered every ounce of power he possessed, straining, grunting, pulling it up onto the tailgate and allowing it to fall over backward into the truck. He pushed and shoved it over to the middle of the truck and then opened the door and lifted the girl and put her inside.

She wouldn't fit.

He put her in head first and then tried closing the door, but she wouldn't fit.

He tried turning her on her side and bending her legs behind her, but that didn't work either. He was beginning to get very nervous because he was afraid someone would turn on a light or open a window or look down into the yard and see him struggling there trying to get the girl into the refrigerator.

He broke both her legs.

He closed the door.

He got into the truck and began driving.

The city was an empty wilderness, he did not know where to go, he did not know where he could leave her. He did not want anyone to find the refrigerator because then they would find the girl and know who she was and possibly they would trace the refrigerator back to Mrs. Dougherty's rooming house and begin to ask questions. He found the river almost be accident. He knew the city was surrounded by water, but it didn't occur to him that he could just drive up to the river's edge and drop the refrigerator in. He had come across a small bridge and looked down and seen lights reflecting in water, and then realized he was looking down into a river and had taken the first left turn off the bridge and driven down to a deserted dock where a railroad car loomed alone and empty on a silent track. He backed the truck to the water's edge. He wondered how deep the water was. He went to the edge of the dock and got down on his hands and knees and looked over to see if there were any markings on the dock, but there weren't. He didn't want to go dropping the refrigerator into shallow water. They'd find it right off, and that wouldn't be too good.

He got into the truck again and drove off.

Now that he knew he wanted to drop the refrigerator in the river, he began actively looking for a place that would be deep enough. He didn't know how he would recognize a deep spot unless he just happened to come across a dock or bridge that was marked. But the chances of finding such a placed seemed

A bridge.

Actually, if he

Well, just drive onto it.

The middle of it.

The rail.

He could simply

He began looking for a bridge. He'd have to be very careful, he'd have to pretend something was wrong, yes, that was it, wait for a break, just bide his time, that refrigerator was very heavy. Yes.

Yes.

He drove crosstown, thinking a high bridge would be best, the refrigerator would drop a very long distance and then sink into the mud on the bottom of the river. Yes, a high bridge would be best. He headed automatically toward the highest and longest bridge he knew, the one connecting the city with the adjoining state, and then he started across it. The bridge seemed to sway somewhat in the strong wind. He wondered if the refrigerator would drop straight and true to the river, or if the wind would affect its fall.

He stopped the truck.

He went immediately to the front and lifted the hood.

He stood in front of the truck as though he were looking into the engine, but he was really watching the far end of the bridge and the approaching headlights. As soon as there was a break in the traffic, he would go to the back and lift the refrigerator down, and carry it behind the side of the truck so that he would be shielded from any other passing cars. He kept watching the cars in the distance. The headlights rushed past.

All at once, there was nothing.

Nothing was coming.

I hope this works, he thought.

He went quickly to the back of the truck, thinking how heavy the refrigerator was going to be and then surprised to find that it was amazingly light, he could lift it with hardly any effort at all. He felt almost a little giddy as he lifted the refrigerator, God it was light, and carried it around the side of the truck and then hoisted it up onto the guard rail. He looked down once quickly, to make sure no boats were passing under the bridge, and then he let the refrigerator drop. He watched it as it went down, leaving his hands large and white and getting smaller and smaller and hitting the water with an enormous splash that sent up a large white geyser of water. A car rushed past in the opposite direction. The water below was settling, a wide circle of white spreading, there were headlights at the far end of the bridge now. He went quickly to the front of the truck and pulled down the hood. He came around the side again and took one last look at the water below.

You could hardly tell anything had been dropped into the river.

He started the truck and drove across the bridge and into the next state. He drove about a mile past the toll booths, and then made a U-turn and headed back for the city. He dropped the truck off at the garage and walked to Mrs. Dougherty's. There was no one outside the building or in the hallway. Everyone was asleep. He went up to his room and got into bed.

He fell asleep almost instantly.

Amelia opened the door.

She had washed her face, and washed the lipstick from her mouth and now she entered the room and closed the door behind her, and carefully and slowly locked it. She put her bag on the dresser, and then turned to face him, leaning against the door with her hands behind her back.

"Hi," she said.

He looked up at her. "Hello."

"Did you miss me?"

"Yes."

"Tell me."

"I missed you."

"You've got some fancy bathroom down the hall there," she said. She did not move from the door. She kept staring at him, a faint strange smile on her face. "Blue toilet paper, very fancy."

"I didn't notice," Roger said.

"You're not a very observant person, are you?" She tripped on only the one word, observant, saying it a little thickly and almost missing it entirely. She wasn't really too drunk, she'd just had a few too many, and she stood inside the locked door with her hands behind her back and that very strange, mischievous, somehow evil smile on her face. He looked at her and thought

how beautiful she was and then thought I'd better get
her out of here before I hurt her.

She moved away from the door.

She came to where he was sitting on the edge of the
bed and she moved very close to him, with her knees
touching his, and then she reached down seriously and
solemnly, with a drunken dignity, and spread her hands
on either side of his head like two open fans. She tilted
his face up and then bent down and kissed him on the
lips, with her own mouth open. He reached up behind
her to cup her buttocks in his huge hands, thinking
how much he wanted to love her, and thinking how his
mother would of course object even though she was very
beautiful. His mother would of course point out that she
was a colored girl. He wondered when it had begun to
matter just what the hell his mother thought about the
girls he went out with, who the hell cared *what* his mother
thought? And then he realized that he'd been caring what
his mother thought for a long long time and that last
night when he had finally said to hell with her, when
he had finally let himself go with Molly, why that was
the bad part, that was why he'd had to do it to her.

To kill her.

I killed her, he thought.

Amelia's mouth was covering him, her tongue was
insistently probing, her lips were thick and soft and wet
and he felt himself falling back onto the bed with her
on top of him, and feeling the softness of her breasts
against his chest, his heart beating wildly. He began
trembling. She had taken off her bra in the bathroom,
he realized she had taken off her bra. His hands moved
swiftly up under her sweater and over her back. He rolled
onto her suddenly, moaning, and kissed her breasts, the
dark swollen nipples. "Oh, Roger," she was saying, "oh
Roger, I love you, I love you."

He was lost in the aroma of her and in the warmth of her and in the dizzy insistence of her mouth, but at the same time he was thinking more clearly than he had since late last night when he had dropped the refrigerator in the river. He was thinking that he had to get her out of here because he was sure he would hurt her. He had hurt Molly without even having liked her at first, had hurt her only later when she somehow got him angry, but he felt a lusting rage now for this girl who was beautiful and "She is colored," his mother would say, "Why are you bringing home a little colored whore to me," he loved her lips and the way her hands she was dangerous if he did not get rid of her they would find out about Molly. If he hurt her, if she allowed him to love her, if she allowed him to enter her the dark pulsing interior of her in his hands now warm and moving against him the smooth dark smothering breasts if she allowed him to love her you're the man in the family now he would have to kill her there would be no other way he would have to kill her, they would find out about Molly, get away from me he thought.

He drew away from her sharply.

She stared up at him.

Her sweater was pulled up over her naked breasts, her skirt was high on her thighs. He crouched over her trembling with love for her. She reached for him tenderly. Her hand came up to him slowly and with infinite gentleness, touching him, assuring him

"No!" he shouted.

"What?"

"Get— No," he said.

He moved off the bed. He turned his back to her.

"Go," he said. "Go home. Get out of here. Get out!"

"What?"

He was at the closet. He opened the door and took

out her coat and brought it to the bed and put it down beside her without looking at her again, knowing she had still not pulled down the sweater, loving her and afraid he would hate her, please, please, go, please, not knowing whether he said the words aloud.

She got off the bed silently. She adjusted her sweater, and silently got into her coat. She picked up her bag from the dresser, went to the door, and unlocked it.

"I'll never as long as I live understand," she said and went out.

It was about seven o'clock when he went down for the truck and drove it over to the police station.

He parked just across the street, pulling up the hand brake and then cutting the ignition and glancing over to where the green globes were lighted now, the 87 showing on each of them, flanking the entrance doors.

He knew he was about to do the right thing.

It seemed very good to him that he had not harmed Amelia. That seemed like a very good sign. He didn't know why he hadn't done this right from the beginning, why he simply hadn't brought Molly here last night, right after he'd killed her, instead of putting her in the refrigerator and throwing her in the river where they'd never find her. He could have told it to someone right then and spared himself all the fear and

Wouldn't they?

Find her?

He sat quite still behind the wheel of the truck with darkness covering the city and with the precinct globes feebly glowing across the street, throwing a pale-green stain on the snow banked along the precinct steps. There was the sound of shovels scraping the sidewalks, tire chains rattling on snow. His breath plumed into the cold cab interior, the windshield was getting frosted.

She had only been in the city a week, no one knew she was here, except of course the hotel she was staying at. She would have signed a register, yes, what was the name of the hotel, a Spanish name. It didn't matter. They would think she'd skipped without paying her bill, that was all. They'd maybe report it to the police, or maybe not, depending on what she'd left behind, didn't she say she'd come here with only a suitcase and a little money, sure. But even if they did report her missing, even if they said Molly Nolan who was staying here at the hotel has just vanished without taking her clothes out of the dresser, well, okay, let's say they did that. Let's say they told the police.

She's at the bottom of the river, Roger thought.

She's not going to float up to the top because she's locked inside a heavy refrigerator, I could barely lift it onto the tailgate of the truck, I dropped that refrigerator maybe a hundred and fifty feet from the bridge to the water, maybe more, I was never good at judging distance. It must have sunk ten feet into the river bottom, or at least five, or even three, it didn't matter. Even if it was just laying there exposed on the bottom it was never going to be found, never. It was just going to sit there forever with Molly Nolan dead inside it, and nobody in the world would ever know she was down there. Her parents were dead, her only friend was in Hawaii, nobody had noticed Roger and her in the bar, nobody had seen them go up to his room together, no one would ever know.

All he had to do was drive away.

No one would ever know.

If he did not go into the police station across the street and tell them he had killed her, why they just would never know about it, they just would never find out.

He looked across the street.

I'd better go tell them, he thought.

He got out of the truck.

He was about to cross the street when the door opened. Two men came out of the station house. He recognized the taller one as the detective he'd followed to the restaurant that afternoon, and he thought, Good, he's the one I wanted to tell this to in the first place. The man with him was bald. Roger supposed he was a detective, too. The green precinct lights shone on his bald head. They gave him a funny appearance.

The men had reached the sidewalk.

Go ahead, Roger thought. Go tell him. He's the one you wanted to tell.

He hesitated.

The one with the bald head ran to the curb and made a snowball and threw it at the taller detective. The taller detective laughed, and then picked up a pile of snow and just flipped it at the bald-headed one in a big lump, without packing it, and they both laughed like kids.

"I'll see you tomorrow," the taller one said, laughing.

"Right, Steve. Good night," the bald-headed one said.

"Good night."

The men walked off in opposite directions.

Roger watched the taller one until he was out of sight.

He got back into the truck and turned the ignition key, starting the engine. He looked at the station house one more time, and then began driving home.

To mother.

SEE THEM DIE

ED MCBAIN

'Kill me if you can' was Pepe Miranda's challenge.

Murderer, two-bit hero of the street gangs, he was holed up somewhere in the 87th Precinct, making the cops look like fools and cheered on by every neighbourhood punk.

Not a challenge Lieutenant Pete Byrnes and the detectives in the squadroom could leave alone.

Not in the sticky July heat of the city with the gangs just itchy with the need to explode into violence.

'The best modern American crime writer.' *Sunday Express*

'Ed McBain is a master. He's virtually reinvented the police procedural novel.' *Newsweek*

HODDER AND STOUGHTON PAPERBACKS